OPERATION SUBVERSION

the **PROMGEN** files

Archives

OPERATION SUBVERSION

Aly Kay Tibbitts

BATTALION PRESS

FARMINGTON, UTAH

Library of Congress Control Number: **2025909441**
ISBN: **978-1-955192-08-8** (Hardcover)
978-1-955192-09-5 (e-Book)
978-1-955192-10-1 (Paperback)

The text type was set in Garamond and Courier New.
Front cover image by Alyx Tibbitts.
Book design by Alyx Tibbitts.

Published by Battalion Press.

First Edition, Sept. 2025

To Mikayli

my real life Emily Nour Hall

TOP SECRET PROMISING GENERATION EYES ONLY

Operation Subversion
Objective: Systematically dismantle the Circle of Fifths

FIELD REPORT:18 October 2000

CLASSIFIED TOP SECRET

15:10 EDT Potomac School; McLean, VA
15:47 EDT McLean Estate; McLean, VA
20:27 PDT LAX; Los Angeles, CA

15:10 EDT
McLean, Virginia
Upper School, Potomac School

SPRING AT THE POTOMAC SCHOOL in McLean Virginia, I was told, was something not to miss. I wouldn't know. I have yet to see a spring in Virginia, but I was having a hard time imagining it could be better than the springs I had spent in Disneyland or on the beach in Southern California.

The current Virginia weather was definitely not better than the weather of my childhood home. The colors were pretty. The temperature was not. Everyone seemed infatuated with the seasons, and complained about California only having one, but I would prefer seeing the sun and feeling its warmth through the winter than having the beauty of *seasons*.

Call me crazy.

I ducked my head, throwing my bag over my shoulder as the bell rang, dismissing me from my last class of the day: English.

As I entered the swarm of students already heading towards the exit, I barely heard the yelled homework assignment: "Read through chapter 7 by tomorrow, and don't forget your essays are due on Monday." With the reminder from Mrs. Henry (my AP English Literature and Composition teacher) already fading from my mind, I knew by the time I got home I would regret not stopping to write it down.

Right now, all I wanted to do was get out of here.

I hiked my backpack up a little further on my shoulder, ducking my head to avoid the gazes of other students. I had already been here for two months, and I had yet to find very many friends, not that I really tried. Everyday, I received strange looks, asking me why I was going the wrong way. I didn't fit in. Everyone else had been here since Kindergarten, and had grown up with each other. They had attended every birthday party, and had thrown several secret ragers. They knew everything there was to know about everyone else, partially from knowing them for so long, and partially because the school was so small, the rumors sped through faster than the Concord. I was new. I was quiet. No one knew me, and I didn't offer to let them get to know me. I was here for one reason, and I didn't care about the rumors that speculated why I had started here at the beginning of the year—my *senior* year.

I finally broke free from the crowd and headed for the nearest door. As I got out of the Upper School building, I took a deep breath, taking in the scent of the woods surrounding the school, and angled myself in the direction of the Lower School to pick up my niece.

When my sister, Sarah, and her husband, Neil, had started discussing Vee starting school in Virginia, so she could live with Neil's parents while he was training for the FBI at Quantico, and Sarah got her Nursing degree, I had been the one to suggest I come with them. I had been the one to find the Potomac School. It was my suggestion that I could attend the same school as my niece, who was starting Kindergarten. If we both attended the same school, I could pick her up from school, so Madelyn, Neil's mother, wouldn't have to do it.

What I hadn't realized was that 90 acres was substantially bigger than the school I had attended in California. Still, I wouldn't complain about the walk from the building that housed my classes over to the playground at the Lower School where Vee would wait for me to come get her. Despite only being three miles from the nation's capital, the air was crisp. On days like today, it was almost enough to make me forget that I didn't own a coat warm enough for the coming winter. It almost made me forget the reason I didn't hesitate to leave my friends behind. It almost made me forget why I had to be here for Vee.

I couldn't help but smile as I approached the playground and noticed my sister watching as Vee flew back and forth across the monkey bars, It had been a while since I'd seen Vee with so much energy and excitement, so I decided to let her continue playing, choosing instead to focus on my sister, who to everyone watching looked like she was Vee's mother, but I knew wasn't. She was so focused on our niece as I walked up that I was able to get right next to her before she noticed me. I pulled a tabloid out of my backpack and read the cover out loud to her. "Trouble in Paradise! Ally and Michael call it quits!"

Ally just rolled her eyes. "You know you can't believe everything you read in those magazines. I thought I taught you better," she said in response.

I nodded. "Yes." I shoved the magazine back in my bag. "But someone hasn't been around to make sure I kept up with my training. Then again, it seems you've gotten soft."

Ally shook her head. "How did you know it was me anyway?"

"Sarah doesn't come to pick up Vee." I replied, tugging my backpack back onto my shoulder again.

"How is she doing?"

"Ok." I glance at Ally. It's weird to be reporting to her how her own twin sister is doing. It made me think I shouldn't be quite so hurt that I didn't hear from Ally so often if she didn't talk to Sarah very often either. Then again, I doubted Ally was to blame for their current lack of communication; Sarah wasn't talking to anyone right now.

For years I'd thought Ally was horrible at communicating, but I had heard more from her since the incident than I had from Sarah, the sister I lived with. I didn't know when the last time was that she talked to Neil.

We were all grieving, but Sarah…

"She's getting her Master's in Nursing from John Hopkins, so she's exhausted."

Ally nodded. "She's throwing herself into work so she doesn't have time to think about what happened." She sighed. "She never did have healthy coping mechanisms. What about Neil?"

"At Quantico. FBI training."

Ally let out a fake gasp. "Traitor!"

I couldn't help but laugh. She had always had an amazing ability to get the people around her to laugh when the didn't feel like it, and I already felt lighter being around her. "Yeah, well, what are we supposed to say about you? Neil changed agencies. You quit and moved countries."

"Fair point." Ally admitted. She turned her head away from Vee, observing me from head to toe. She put her arm around me giving me a hug. "It's been a while Em. You're taller than I remember."

"I was on the floor playing with the kids the last time you saw me," I reminded her. "Someone keeps using me for free baby-sitting for Feilds' Ball instead of letting me attend with the rest of my siblings."

She nodded. "I know. I'm sorry. This year, I promise I will find someone to watch the kids. Cole is old enough—" She stopped, catching herself. "I'll find someone."

I looked at Ally as she returned her attention to Vee, watching her for a few minutes. Everything Ally had done to help me forget the tragedy that had brought me here lost its efficacy. I still had Vee, but she was missing her siblings. I could never fill that void for her. It was hard for me too, seeing her everyday and being reminded of the niece and nephew I'd lost. I didn't like the way Sarah and Neil were coping with the loss, but I couldn't imagine what they were going through.

"I'm surprised she's doing so well." Ally finally said.

"This is actually the happiest I've seen her in a while. I think she's just too young to understand. Yesterday, she was telling me what happened again, but she changed the story, saying I was the one that went with her, and that she saw me sneak out the back door before—you know. She's changing the story so everyone survives."

"Maybe Annie did." Ally commented. "Alyx is young, so no one has pushed to get a complete statement from her. She shuts down, we give up."

I pulled away from my sister. "No. Annie didn't survive. Vee has told us what happened to the best of her ability, and she gave us a pretty good statement for being *five*."

"So she has the ability to give an accurate statement to the police mere hours after the explosion, but after she has had time to process everything she's seen, you are going to discount what she tells you as a *story*?" Ally criticized. "If we are going to say she is a reliable witness, we have to consider *every* version of the story she tells. Annie escaping before the explosion makes more sense with the evidence they found in the house. They didn't recover their bodies."

"I know you weren't there, but they didn't find their bodies because the fire was so hot. *No one* could have survived that, never mind a couple of kids." I argued.

Ally sighed. "Do you know why the police didn't do anything with Alyx' confession?"

"Because she's five. She doesn't understand the difference between guilty and survivor's guilt."

Ally shook her head. "They found the bodies of the people Alyx said she saw in the house. They identified the ignition point, and it's clear that the bodies they found were the people responsible for starting the fire." Ally turned to look at me. I could tell she was trying to study my face and see if I understood what she was telling me. I didn't. She took a deep breath before continuing. "Cole survived."

She had said it so quietly I almost didn't hear her. I stared at her. There was no way I'd heard her correctly.

"He showed up at Feilds Palace after the funeral. He explained to me what he remembered from that day. Someone pulled him from the house, then went back inside for Annie. He climbed up in the tree house next door to see when Annie came out, but the explosion knocked him back and he hit his head. By the time he woke up, everyone thought he was dead, so he made his way to me. He wants me to train him to be better so he can protect Alyx next time." Ally explained.

She had said what I thought she had. I was speechless. I had been watching as Sarah fell apart. When the kids didn't come back from their bike ride she went out looking for them. She had buckled Cassie into her carseat, and started driving around the streets where they usually rode. When she saw the firetrucks, she assumed the worst and followed them. She arrived right before the explosion. She saw their bikes dumped in the neighbor's yard. She saw Vee come running from the burning house. She heard Vee say her siblings went inside with her, but she didn't know where they were; she lost them in the fire.

Sarah had been nothing but a helpless spectator as the house her children were in exploded.

I pulled my Nokia out of my backpack, using the light blue button on the top of the phone to turn it on.

"What are you doing?" Ally asked me.

"Calling Sarah. She deserves to know."

Sarah deserved to know she hadn't failed Cole.

Ally pulled the phone away from me before I had a chance to dial Sarah's phone number. "We can't tell Sarah. Cole found something in that house. I need to take care of it."

I walked closer to the playground. If Ally was going to keep secrets from Sarah, I didn't want to be part of it. The more she told me and asked me not to tell Sarah, the more difficult my life would be. "Vee, come on. Let's go home." I called.

"Just a little longer Em?" She called back. It broke my heart, tearing her away from something that made her so happy, but I knew we needed to get back to her grandparents' house so both of us could start homework. *Chapter 7. Essay.* I chanted my home work assignment over and over again in my head as a reminder.

I also didn't want to talk to my sister any longer. I would have to listen to her if I let Vee stay and play longer.

"That's why I'm here, Emily. I need your help." Ally said behind me. "I also want to find out if Annie is alive. I don't want to give them a sense of false hope that she might be."

I glanced back at Ally. Her face was sincere. It was hurting her too, not telling her twin sister that Cole was alive.

I sighed. "Five minutes." I replied to Vee, then turned to my older sister. "You have the same amount of time."

"It was Circle of Fifths." Ally said.

"I know." I replied. "Who else would come after Sarah and her kids like this? Especially five years after they killed dad. Neil's dad thinks they used the CIA database to figure out where Sarah and Neil were living."

"They didn't use the database." Ally said. "They weren't trying to kill the kids. Alyx wasn't lured inside. Cole said it looked like they had been using that house for months, if not years. He saw files on all the kids of the Promising Generation Program. Those aren't on the CIA database. And the reason the house exploded was because they were found."

"Are you saying…" I trailed off, not wanting to finish what I was going to say. I knew how to access the files that Ally was talking about, and I desperately didn't want to be right. If I was right, things were a lot worse than we had all thought they were.

"The Circle of Fifths is imbedded on Sarah's team. Possibly even imbedded in the Promising Generation Program." Ally finished.

"Who?" I asked. Vee wouldn't be safe if we didn't know who was imbedded, and neither would any of the other kids. I had helped trained most of them. Sarah and Neil had the resources to disappear, and make sure Vee stayed hidden too. But the rest of the Promising Generation? They were just as innocent as Vee was.

"That's what I need your help with," Ally admitted. "You still have access to the files. I need help figuring out who the double agent is so we can take them down."

I looked over at the playground, and the five-year old that had already lost so much in her short life. She was now in as much danger as any of the adults who had dedicated their lives to finding the Circle of Fifths, and she hadn't done anything. If helping Ally meant I could give that little girl a chance at a normal childhood, and still live to see adulthood, I would. So I nodded. "Let me get her home, then we can talk about what you need me to do." I said.

"You guys are staying with Deputy Director McLean, right?" Ally asked.

"Yeah. With Neil at Quantico, and Sarah spending most of her time at school, they figured that would be the safest option for Vee."

"And you?" Ally asked as she walked with me to the monkey bars where Vee was still playing. "Why did you follow them out here when you didn't have to?"

I shrugged, focusing my attention on Vee instead of answering Ally's question. "Come on Vee. Time to go." I could have told her that I wasn't eighteen yet, so I had to have a guardian. Sarah and Neil had moved back to the house we grew up in to take care of it and became my de-facto guardians five years ago.

Maybe I didn't want to stay in that stupid house while yet another tragedy sent my family running from ghosts.

As much as I didn't want to admit it, though, I knew it was just an excuse, and not a very good one at that. If I had wanted to, Sarah would have let me stay in Chino Hills. I was old enough to take care of myself. I was months away from turning eighteen, and being a legal adult.

Any excuse I could have given would have been a lie. They would ignore the fact that coming with Vee had been my idea.

"Please Emily?" Vee whined.

"I already gave you more time." I told her.

"But I have to keep training." Vee explained.

I shook my head. "Alyxandrie Madelyn McLean. We need to go home. *Training* is not more important than learning."

Vee dropped down off the monkey bars, landing with a grace that few five-year-olds were capable of demonstrating. "But Cole and Annie won't come home until I'm strong enough. I want to be strong enough so they come home."

I shot a dirty look at Ally. Cole could have been right here, next to his little sister, taking care of her like he had since the day she was born. I wanted to tell Vee that her brother, her protector, would be home soon, but I could tell from my conversation with Ally he wouldn't. Just like Vee was trying to be strong enough her siblings could come home, Cole was trying to become strong enough to protect Vee from anyone who might come after her.

But trying to explain that was much harder than telling her the same thing I'd told her the day before. And the day before that. And everyday since the explosion.

I kneeled down, bringing my eyes level to Vee's. I put my hands on her tiny arms. "Alyx," I started, using the shortened version of her name that everyone else used, instead of the nickname I called her. "If Cole and Annie could, they would be at home with you." I said. "They aren't waiting for you to be stronger. That's not why they're not here."

"But, but I wasn't strong enough. They had to save me and that's why they're gone. I'm why they're dead. I killed them." Vee answered.

I took a deep breath. It didn't matter how many times I heard Vee take the blame for killing her siblings, every time she said those words, my heart hurt. I couldn't imagine what this little girl was going through. She thought it was her fault. She felt guilty, and I couldn't take that guilt away, or explain to her why what she was feeling was survivor's guilt, not guilt for doing something bad.

I was missing my niece and nephew, but I still had all my siblings.

"Vee, remember what I told you about saying that? You didn't kill them. It's not your fault. And we don't say that, ok?" I waited for her to nod. "Ok. Let's go home." I reached out for her hand, which, thankfully, she took without any more prodding. "Where is your backpack?"

She pointed to the base of the monkey bars.

"Ok, let's go get it." I said, walking with her over to get it. Instead of putting it on her back, however, I just grabbed the top handle with my free hand, and turned back towards the Upper School, where the parking lot was with my car.

"Is Ally coming with us?" Vee asked.

I snickered, looking back at Ally. Even this five-year-old was able to tell her mom apart from her identical twin.

"Ok," Ally said, frustrated. "How do you know I'm Ally, and not your mom?" She asked.

Vee shrugged. "I dunno. Just do. I like you more than mom though. We explore Feilds Palace together. Are we going to explore Feilds Palace?"

Ally gave a sad smile. "Not right now. Maybe when you come visit next summer."

"Sorry Ally." I teased. "This little one might actually be smarter than you." I moved the hand holding Vee's hand back and forth to show Ally who I was talking about, even though I knew she knew.

15:47 EDT
McLean, Virginia
McLean Residence

ALLY'S CAR WAS ALREADY IN front of the McLean's house when I parked my car out front. If it weren't for the diplomatic plates on the car, I probably would have questioned whether or not my sister had actually beat me back to the house that had become my home. Then again, I did have an extremely active five-year-old that I had to not only get to my car, but also get both of our backpacks in the car, and her in her car seat.

Correction: it's a booster seat. Not a car seat. Vee always corrects me when I call it a car seat.

She liked to think she was big enough that she could get her seatbelt on herself, but I always had to help her tighten it. So, while I was surprised, it made sense that Ally was able to leave the school with a decent head-start on me.

I used the key I'd been given to let Vee and I into her grandparent's house. I felt weird when they had first given me a key, because I wasn't technically related to the McLeans. I was their son's wife's sister. Mrs. McLean, Vee's grandma (who had insisted

I call her Madelyn), had told me that I was family, just as much as Sarah. I eventually reasoned myself into believing them. Sarah and Neil had, after all, practically raised me after they'd gotten married. If I looked at Sarah and Neil as parent figures (and they were technically my guardians), it was easy to convince myself that yes, Madelyn was just as much my family as she was Sarah's.

What I hadn't realized, was that Ally was also very close to Neil's parents. When Vee and I walked into the house, we found Madelyn very amicably catching up with Ally, who despite not stepping foot in the United States, never mind this house, for the past decade, looked like she belonged in the house just as much as the rest of us did.

Madelyn looked at Vee and I as we walked into the house. She tried to catch Vee for a hug as she trudged past her grandmother and aunt, but she wasn't having it. The energy and excitement she'd shown on the playground at school had slowly disappeared on the drive home, until she had returned to the little girl she'd become the day her siblings died. She was much too serious for her own good.

"Alyx, how was school?" Madelyn asked.

Vee shrugged. Ally looked at me, her eyes asking what happened on the way home, but Madelyn was used to seeing Vee this way.

"She was really excited before we left the school. Happier than I've seen her in a while." I told Madelyn. "I think school really helps her."

Madelyn nodded. "Alyx, come here." As Vee came over, Madelyn bent her knees, bringing her face down low enough that she was about the same height as Vee. She put her hands on Vee's elbows, looking in her eyes as she talked. "What did you learn at school today?"

Vee's face brightened a bit. "We learned about vowels today. I like the letter *A* because my name starts with it, but I also like *Y*, cuz sometimes it's a vowel, but sometimes it's not, and I think that's cool."

"Yeah?" Madelyn asked, showing interest in what she was saying with the skill that only a grandmother could. "My name has a *Y* in it. So does Ally's name and Emily's. But you're really lucky because you have a *Y* in both your first *and* middle name. Did you know that?"

Vee shook her head. "I knew my name did, but not yours or Ally's."

"Yeah. Why don't we go practice writing our names so we can see the *Y*?" Madelyn suggested.

Vee brightened even more with this suggestion, taking her grandmother's hand. I handed Madelyn Vee's backpack, and the two of them walked back to the kitchen. As they left, Ally looked at me, letting me know it was no mistake that Madelyn found a way to get Vee out of the room. "Should we go to my room?" I asked her.

Ally nodded. "I think that sounds like a good idea."

I led Ally upstairs to the room that had become mine two months before. I opened the door, turning on the light, and dropping my backpack next to the small school desk right next to the door, complete with a blue chair that looked just like the chairs they had in Vee's kindergarten classroom. I went over to the bed, a bunkbed with a double bed on the bottom and a twin above it, and sat down on the neatly made bottom bunk.

Ally stayed in the doorway, looking around the room. I watched as she took in the desk at the foot of the bed with the computer on it, the small desk by the door with the French worksheets on it, the bunk bed, and slowly started to put it all together.

"You share a room with Alyx." She said. "Why?"

"I don't want to impose." I replied.

Ally shook her head. "You know I taught you how to lie." She looked up on the top bunk, seeing it so covered in all of Vee's stuffed animals it was clear she hadn't slept in the bed for quite some time.

"She has nightmares. She tried to climb in bed with her parents at first, but Neil isn't here, and Sarah can't really sleep either. Plus with her classes, she is usually up late studying—if she even comes home. I think she found a place closer to school to stay for now." I explain the unasked question I hear hanging in the air. "Now Vee usually just climbs in bed with me."

"She's the reason you moved for senior year." Ally said, answering her own question that I had left unanswered back at the school. She nodded. "I'm glad she has someone to look out for her still. She needs that."

"I know." I replied softly.

"I'm heading to Chino Hills." Ally told me, seamlessly transitioning into the conversation we came to this room to have.

"Ally—"

"Michael and I have a visit scheduled. I want you to come with us." Ally said.

I shook my head. "Do you have any idea how dangerous that is?" I asked her. "I mean, even I know that the danger is the real reason Sarah and Neil moved themselves and Vee here. For all we know, it's too dangerous for me to go back, and I haven't done anything to piss off the Circle of Fifths. At least not the way you or Sarah have. But you're a public figure. You don't just have the Circle of Fifths to worry about, you have to worry about the danger your title puts you and Michael in."

"The title belongs to Michael, not me." Ally corrected.

I waved my hand in dismissal, caring more about my argument than the intricacies of the British Peerage system. "Same difference. The point is, Michael has a courtesy title, and will receive his father's title, and because of that, you are Lady Ally Hall Feilds. You have a target painted on you, one way or the other."

Ally raised an eyebrow. "You've done your research."

I shrugged, looking at the stack of tabloids on the bookshelf that Vee and I shared. "I had to do something to feel close to you. London is really far away when you are ten and can't travel by yourself."

Ally turned to see what I was looking at, seeing the tabloids that had become my obsession since she left and married Michael. "Well…" she started, crossing the room and sitting next to me on my bed. "I'm sure your precious tabloids haven't mentioned that with the title comes a very large, and quite skilled army of security."

I glanced around the room. "Are they invisible too?"

This caused a laugh from Ally. "No. I figured it would be better for me to fly under the radar to come talk to you. Michael had a stop to make in DC, so it was easier if I disappeared for a few hours anyway."

"Can you really say they're skilled if you were able to sneak away?" I asked.

Ally smirked. "Trust me, they're good. And MI:6 spared no expense for our security. They have reserved us a presidential suite in LA. However, given the current security risk, I was able to convince my father-in-law that we should use one of the Hall safehouses. We are planning on using decoys at the hotel, while Michael and I stay off the grid at the safehouse."

"If it's that dangerous for you to go, why are you?" I asked.

"I already told you why. I need you to use your New Generation Database access to figure out who in the team is Circle of Fifths."

"That explains why I need to go to Chino Hills, not why you do," I retorted, but failed to correct her assumption that I had access to the New Generation Database.

Technically, I had access to the Promising Generation Database, not the New Generation Database, since I wasn't yet old enough to join the CIA. Given the circumstances, the distinction wasn't important. It wasn't *any* agent on the New Generation Task Force who had the necessary access to the Promising Generation Database in order to compile the dossiers Ally had described—only parents of children in the Promising Generation had that kind of access. If I argued the distinction though, Ally might leave before I could explain why she needed me. The important part was the fact that either database could only be accessed *in person*, and that meant traveling to our Head Quarters in Los Angeles.

"Once you find out who it is, I want to take care of it." Ally said. "Most of Sarah's task force is still stationed in Chino Hills, I believe."

I shake my head. "You shouldn't be risking yourself to root out the mole."

"I'm the only one who can." Ally argued.

"No, you're not. I can do it." I replied. "I have been training for this since I was younger than Vee is. And I know everyone in the New Generation. I have been working with them and their kids in the Promising Generation Program. Besides, if you have a scheduled visit, it would look suspicious if you deviated from your itinerary, which I'm assuming can be found if the right people know where to look. They'll be distracted with yours and Michael's visit. No one will be paying attention to me."

Ally sighed, but she didn't immediately argue, so I knew she was thinking about it. I was halfway to convincing Ally to let me do my part to protect the family.

"Ally, we have the advantage of them not knowing that we are onto them. They think Cole and Annie are dead, and if they are on the New Generation team, then they have read Vee's statement, and they know she didn't see anything." I persuaded. "*I. Can. Do. This.*"

"Fine, but you will tell me when you figure out who it is, and let me know when you are going to talk to them." Ally bargained.

"Deal." I agreed.

"And if anything goes wrong, or you need any back-up, you call me immediately."

"Absolutely," I said. "When do we leave?"

"Tonight." Ally replied.

"Someone is going to have to excuse me from school." I said, the implied question hanging in the air.

Ally nodded with a smile. "Hi, this is Sarah McLean, Emily Hall's guardian. She seems to have come down with something. She has a fever and a sore throat…"

I shrugged. "Sounds convincing to me."

20:27 PDT
Los Angeles, California
LAX

THE MOMENT I GOT OFF the plane, I felt at home. Everything was so familiar: the weather, the feel of the sun on my skin, the smell of the air, and the tingle of the breeze as it passed over the hairs on my arm. I hadn't realized how much I missed it until that moment.

Ally handed me a key and a sealed document envelope as we stood on the tarmac. "I arranged for one of mom and dad's cars to be brought." She told me, before turning and walking toward the car that was being loaded with hers and Michael's luggage. Michael stood at the open door, his hand outstretched towards Ally; his intention to help her in the car first was clear. She took her husband's hand, but then stopped, turning back to look at me. "As soon as you figure out who it is, let me know. I'll have my phone on me."

"I will," I promise. "I'll send you a smily face to let you know I know who it is and need to meet."

"A smily face?" Ally asked.

"Yeah," I said. "A text message with a colon and a parenthesis."

Ally shook her head, getting in the car. "Kids these days."

I smiled at my sister, biting my tongue to stop me from retaliating by calling her old, because she wasn't. Not really. She had just spent too long in London, sheltered behind the security her husband's title required. "What safehouse are you guys staying at?"

"Faultline." Ally replied.

I nodded. One word was all I needed to know exactly where she and Michael were staying. If I knew my sister, I could probably predict the evasive maneuvers they would take to get there too. I watched as Michael closed the door for her, walking around to the other door to get in. He waved the driver away, telling him he could get his own door.

By the time they arrived at the safehouse, it would just be Ally and Michael, no drivers, no security. It was safer for them that way. If no one knew where they were, they couldn't be attacked.

While Michael and the driver got in the car, Ally rolled her window down. "Hey Em!" She called, stopping me from turning to find the car she'd had brought for me.

"Yeah?" I asked.

"Be careful," she pleaded. "Please, please. Be careful."

I nodded. "I will."

The driver started the car, making Ally holler her last reply to me: "You better!"

TOP SECRET PROMISING GENERATION EYES ONLY

Operation Subversion
Objective: Systematically dismantle the Circle of Fifths

FIELD REPORT:19 October 2000

CLASSIFIED TOP SECRET

08:27 PDT New Generation HQ; Los Angeles, CA
09:42 PDT Hall Home; Chino Hills, CA
10:08 PDT Feilds Prep; Chino Hills, CA
11:22 PDT Hidden Trails Elementary; Chino Hills, CA
13:51 PDT Hidden Trails Elementary; Chino Hills, CA
17:49 PDT Faultline; Chino Hills, CA
19:14 PDT Stevens House; Chino Hills, CA
19:32 PDT Stevens House; Chino Hills, CA
20:16 PDT Hall Home; Chino Hills, CA
20:24 PDT Faultline; Chino Hills, CA
21:06 PDT McKenzie House; Chino Hills, CA
21:54 PDT Chino Hills, CA

08:27 PDT
Los Angeles, California
New Generation Head Quarters

I NODDED TO THE GUARD sitting inside the hidden door that led to the New Generation Head Quarters. It may have been a few months since I'd been here, but before the attack, I had been here every day. I didn't technically have a job with the CIA, but I was well on my way to achieving that goal once I turned eighteen.

Sarah and I had created the Promising Generation Program, and had hired the kids of the agents on the New Generation team as *Interns.* The classification as intern didn't grant us a security clearance, which meant we couldn't access most of the New Generation Head Quarters, but Sarah had thought it was important we learn protocols of secure facilities, and thus the PGP floor came to be. CIA blueprints listed most of the first floor as a training facility, and in a way, it was. As they got older and took on more responsibility, they slowly gained more access to the PGP floor.

As the current director of the Promising Generation, I had access to the entire floor, including the server room, where all of the Promising Generation Files were kept.

I slid my security access card on the lock next to the Server Room door, watching as the little light at the top flashed from red to green, telling me I could pull the door open. I checked over both shoulders as I opened the door, making sure no one was around to try and push their way in with me, then slipped in the door, ensuring it closed behind me. No one else had access to this room, so I knew it was a safe place to do my research.

I looked around the room. The east wall was glowing from the various LEDs that flashed on the tall computers that housed the Promising Generation Server. There was a monitor on a table at the back that was connected to the server; few people had a username and password.

I walked over to the computer, set down the envelope Ally had given me next to it, and in typed mine. As the computer was booting up, I opened the envelope, pulling out a pile of papers. Based on the first page, it seemed like an Incident Report. The formatting was identical to what was taught to the members of the Promising Generation. I flipped through pages to find the codename signature on the last page. *Diamondback.*

My smile was immediate as I read the last page. I had already suspected that this was Cole's statement about what happened, but this confirmed it. As a little boy, he'd been obsessed with snakes. When Sarah and I had started the Promising Generation, and offered Cole membership, he asked if he could choose his codename. I could still remember Sarah asking what he wanted his codename to be. *Diamondback. Just because I'm young, and I don't have my rattle yet, doesn't mean I can't be dangerous.*

Sarah and Neil certainly have their hands full with their kids. They are just like them.

Had. Were.

My smile disappeared, remembering why I was here to begin with. I flipped back to the first page, and started reading. I needed to know everything he saw in that house if I was going to be able to find the mole.

TOP SECRET PROMISING GENERATION EYES ONLY

INCIDENT REPORT: 12 JULY 2000
CLASSIFIED TOP SECRET

[TS//PG] 24 July 2000, off-duty Promising Generation Members Diamondback, Lupopecora, and Morningstar, who were exploring around the neighborhood on their bicycles, decided to ride to the end of the cul-de-sac on Ridgegate Drive. As they approached the end on the street, Morningstar told the other two agents that "Bad guys live there" pointing at the house at the very end of the street.

[TS//PG] Despite warnings from Diamondback and Lupopecora, Morningstar threw down their bicycle, and ran towards the house, where Morningstar rang the door bell. When the resident of the house opened the door, Morningstar told him "I know you're a bad guy. I'm here to stop you." The resident proved Morningstar right by pulling Morningstar into the house.

[TS//PG] Concerned for Morningstar's safety, Diamondback and Lupopecora found an open window on the front of the house, and climbed in. By the time they had entered the house, they couldn't tell where Morningstar had gone, causing Diamondback and Lupopecora to perform a careful search of the house for Morningstar.

[TS//PG] While searching the house for Morningstar, Diamondback and Lupopecora both discovered more evidence that Morningstar's assessment of the house had been correct. Various documents were discovered with the Circle of Fifths logo on them, but no attempts to read the documents were made, because Diamondback and Lupopecora smelled smoke. They followed the smell of smoke to the basement, where they located Morningstar tied to a chair in the center of the room while two enemy agents were lighting files on fire.

[TS//PG] Diamondback and Lupopecora took a step back, allowing themselves to come up with a plan to rescue Morningstar. Lupopecora volunteered to act as a distraction, and draw away the enemy agents. Due to the time crunch, Diamondback reluctantly agreed. Diamondback found a hiding spot which would allow them to go unseen as the enemy agents chased Lupopecora. Lupopecora returned to where they had seen files with the Circle of Fifths logo on it to grab one to use as bait to get the enemy agents to give chase.

[TS//PG] With all of the aspects of their plan in place, Lupopecora shouted at the enemy agents, drawing their attention away from Morningstar. Lupopecora then ran, directing them away from Morningstar, and Diamondback. Once the enemy agents were clear of the room, Diamondback entered the room and untied Morningstar. Morningstar told Diamondback "the bad guys have files on us and our friends." Once Morningstar was untied, Diamondback asked Morningstar to take them to the files mentioned. Morningstar took Diamondback's hand, and walked them to an adjacent room that was a bunker, where Diamondback found personnel files for all of the Promising Generation Members, with details about their lives, training, languages spoken, weaknesses, and more, dating back to September 1998.

I paused reading the file. I grabbed a pen that I stuck in my back pocket, and scribbled *September 1998* on the inside flap of the envelop. When I started searching the Generation Files, I knew that I would want to take a close look at anyone who joined the Generation that month.

[TS//PG] After finding the files, Diamondback knew that they needed to get out of the house as soon as possible, and report the breach to Aphrodite and Ducaspie. However, before Diamondback was able to get Morningstar out of the house, Lupopecora returned covered in soot, looking horrified moments before an explosion rocked the house.

[TS//PG] According to Lupopecora, the enemy agents had decided that the threat posed by both Morningstar and Lupopecora was too high, and had initiated the self-destruct sequence. The mechanism malfunctioned, lighting the enemy agents who triggered it on fire.

[TS//PG] The fire spread quickly, causing a beam to fall. The beam separated Morningstar from Diamondback and Lupopecora. Diamondback told Morningstar to run. Lupopecora found a window to try and break for them to escape out of when a second explosion rocked the house.

[TS//PG] While Lupopecora and Diamondback were trying to find a way out of the house, CIA Officer Elisabeth Stevens showed up in the doorway, pulled Diamondback out of the room, and carried Diamondback out of the house before returning to pull out Lupopecora. Diamondback climbed into the treehouse of the house next door to the Circle of Fifths house to have a better view of what was going on.

[TS//PG] Diamondback is unsure of the fate of Lupopecora and Officer Stevens, as a second explosion rocked the house, and the shock of the blast knocked Diamondback into a wall of the tree house. Diamondback didn't recover until Police and Firefighters were already at the scene.

```
[TS//PG] It is Diamondback's recommendation that
an investigation be opened to find the mole in the
Promising Generation may be to prevent future
incidents. Officer Steven's knowledge of the house
that allowed her to locate Diamondback and
Lupopecora might prove she is the mole. However,
her loyalty might be malleable, as evidenced by her
attempt at rescuing Diamondback and Lupopecora.
```

"I will find the mole. I promise." I whispered to Cole.

He had given me plenty of information to start my search. He was right in his analysis of Officer Stevens. She lived further from the house mentioned in the incident than Sarah had. The timing of her arrival and subsequent rescue of Cole suggested she had been notified of a breach and was on her way almost as soon as the kids had shown up. It wasn't a coincidence. Sarah and I had gotten there just before Vee ran out of the house, and we were already out looking for the kids when we heard the sirens.

I knew Officer Stevens, but I knew her son better. He was a bright and talented kid. When he had tested to enter the program, he had almost tested high enough to be classified as a Gold Agent. To date, only Cole, Annie, Thane, Vee, and I had tested high enough to be classified Gold Agents, but for a minute there, I thought it was going to be more than just Halls in Gold. Sarah and I had been ready to give him a Gold classification too until his dad had insisted he was only a Silver Agent.

His code name was Mercury.

I pulled up the roster of Promising Generation members, and found Mercury on the roster to confirm his Recruitment date.

May 1999.

Mercury wasn't the Promising Generation Member I was looking for. As suspicious as his mom's appearance at the Circle of Fifths safehouse was, she wasn't the only mole in the program.

So many explicatives. I won't think them, because then I'd say them, and then Vee will start saying them…

I scrolled through to find the batch of Promising Generation members recruited in September of 1998. There were three. Demeter, Hades, and Clio. Now to figure out which of those three had parents who were Circle of Fifths agents.

This was the point where the files would no longer be useful. When Sarah and I had started the Promising Generation, I had insisted we couldn't keep any more information than necessary on each of our members. We wanted to keep the Promising Generation safe from the Circle of Fifths, but they weaseled their way into so many secure places. There was no guarantee they wouldn't try to gain access to the Promising Generation. The Circle of Fifths prayed on easily manipulated members of the intelligence community. The last thing we needed was having a roster of children, who would eventually enter the intelligence community. Children were malleable, and were the perfect target of the Circle of Fifths tactics.

We had to have a roster, but the roster didn't have to be complete.

Each time a new member joined, they chose a codename they would be known as in our files, we assigned them a PIN that would act as a second level of verification if they called in for help, and they were filtered into a class based on talent, and what kind of career they eventually wanted at the agency. Besides their recruitment date, that was the only information kept on the roster. That was the only reason why I wasn't concerned about the Circle of Fifths having files on the kids. In the program, they only went by their code names, and there was no way they could connect the individual to the code name.

I, on the other hand, knew much more than that. I was a walking, talking encyclopedia of the Promising Generation. I knew which members were related, and I knew who their parents were. I knew where they lived. Both Demeter and Clio had older siblings who were also members, meaning their parents would have had access to the Promising Generation to start making observations of the members before September 1998.

Hades was an only child.

I knew his mom. She may have been older than me by a few years, but I was friends with her. She and her husband had both been on Sarah's team.

So much for hoping there was just one mole.

09:42 PDT
Chino Hills, California
Hall Home

I WAITED UNTIL I HAD parked my car in the garage of the house I'd grown up in before I texted Ally a smiley face. I couldn't take my phone with me into the New Generation Headquarters, and I didn't want to leave myself exposed to an attack while I was distracted and sending the message in the parking lot.

Before I had unlocked the man door to enter the house, my phone started ringing, the pixilated name on the screen telling me that it was Ally calling. I hit the green phone button on the left side of the phone, shoving it between my shoulder and my ear as I walked into the house. "That was fast."

"We had a break in meetings." Ally replied. "What did you find out?"

"There are at least two moles. Possibly four." I replied, moving my hand to replace my shoulder as I entered the house, keeping my eyes peeled. Until I had slept here last night, it had been a while since anyone had been here, and I wanted to make sure I wasn't walking into a Circle of Fifths trap.

"Zut," Ally said on the other end.

That was something I should try. I spoke French, but I had never considered using French expressions of displeasure instead of the other swear words I wanted to use sometimes. French had a lot of words that could express unhappiness, but weren't technically *swear* words, so it wouldn't be the end of the world if Vee picked them up.

"How do you know? And who are they?" Ally asked.

I shook my head. "You've been out of the game too long if you think I am going to tell you over the phone." I paused for a moment. "Where do you want to meet?"

"Michael and I are attending meetings for the next several hours at the school." Ally replied.

Vague. I knew what she meant, which was the point. "I'll come find you, assuming you will be able to step away to talk to me."

"I'm due for a bathroom break." Ally told me.

I smiled. "À tout à l'heure," I said as I hung up. My smile disappeared as I set my stuff down on the island in the kitchen, and saw the list of names I had made of potential moles.

Once I talked to Ally, I planned on arranging a meeting with Officer Stevens. Cole's description of what she had done to rescue him meant approaching her might mean flipping her. If I could develop her as an asset, we could use her as a source of intel in the Circle of Fifths. That would be more valuable than anything we had been able to get on the Circle of Fifths so far.

At the very least, if I flipped her, I would be able to get a definitive list of moles in the New Generation. What to do with that list once we had it was beyond my responsibility, but I knew we couldn't just remove all of the agents from the New Generation. That would tell the Circle of Fifths we were onto them.

I took a deep breath, closing my eyes. I was running straight off a cliff. I needed to slow down and take one step at a time. First, I needed to talk to Ally, then see if Officer Stevens would meet me. Once I got to that point, I could evaluate my options, and take the next step.

10:08 PDT
Chino Hills, California
Feilds Prep Build Site

IF NOT FOR THE SERIOUS reason we were meeting, I would have laughed as I watched Ally, in her sleek business attire and sensible heels, step into the portable restroom that had been brought to the construction site. Knowing how she was dressed, no one would expect her to be here.

And based on the smell, I didn't *want* to be here. But the smell made the porta-potty the best place for us to talk, and not be overheard. No one wanted to be lurking around, and the smell would deter those who wanted to eavesdrop.

"What did you find out?"

Ally asked the same question she had when she had answered the phone earlier, but I knew she was looking for more specifics this time. She wanted me to tell her what I wouldn't say over the phone earlier.

And I was happy to oblige her. I wanted to brag. At least a little.

"Cole's report made a suggestion about Officer Stevens, and I have to agree. Her presence in the safehouse is a strong indication that she is Circle of Fifths. She has one son in the program, so it makes sense that she would be the mole." I reported.

"But on the phone you said there are at least two," Ally commented.

I nodded. "Cole's report also made a very important observation about how far back the Circle of Fifths had information on the Promising Generation. Cole said the information dated back to September 98. Steven's son didn't join until May of 99…"

"Meaning she wouldn't have had access until he joined the program. Someone else is also involved," Ally finished. "Do you know who?"

"I know whose parents *could* be the mole." I replied. "Cole's report suggests that Stevens might not be entirely loyal to the Circle of Fifths, so I figure I will go talk to her, and see if I can turn her. If I can, hopefully she can confirm who else is involved."

"Emily…" Ally said, a warning tone in her voice.

"I know how to turn an asset," I reminded her. "I already have the basis of a relationship with her. I know what to say to make her think meeting is her idea, and I know what questions to ask to judge her willingness to share information about the Circle of Fifths. I was born to do this, just like you."

"It's not just you who will be in danger if you say the wrong thing, and she isn't willing to turn against the Circle of Fifths," Ally warns me. "She will know that you suspect her involvement, and she is smart enough to figure out how."

I took a deep breath as I thought about what Ally was trying to tell me. If I couldn't turn Officer Stevens, and she figured out that I wanted to, she would figure out that Cole is alive. Vee was currently being hunted by the Circle of Fifths. Cole was not, but only because everyone thought he was dead.

"I'll be careful," I promised, and I meant it. I wouldn't do anything to put my nephew in danger. I couldn't.

Ally looked at her watch. "When do you plan to meet her?"

I shook my head. "I don't know. I know where her son goes to school, and I know she leaves work early on Thursdays to volunteer in his classroom. I'll text you a *6* when I see her, and a smiley face when I leave, so you know I'm safe, how about that?"

"Perfect." Ally replied, her desire to make sure I was safe satisfied. "Meet me for dinner at the safehouse tonight to report."

With her last order given, she stepped back out of the portable restroom, and walked back towards the school that she and her husband were funding. The hope was that once it was completed, the Private School could be used as the perfect cover for expanding the Promising Generation. I already planned on returning to California for college, and attending somewhere in So Cal so I could help.

But before we could open the school, we needed to make sure we didn't have any more moles. We had to keep the kids safe.

11:22 PDT
Chino Hills, California
Hidden Trails Elementary School

IT WAS UNFAIR HOW NORMAL and unchanged the elementary school looked. As I pulled up and parked in the small parking lot, I had flashbacks to every time I'd been here before.

Considering Cole, Analyn, and I had all attended here, I had been here a lot.

The flashbacks of my niece and nephew were painful, and returning from them was even worse. I took several calming breaths and closed the door of the car Ally had arranged for me, and started walking towards the front office. I hiked my backpack up on my shoulder as I approached the door of the office. It didn't matter how many years had passed since I was last a student here, or how many other schools I attended, I would always feel like a small child on this campus.

I smiled at the secretaries as I walked into the office and approached the front counter. I knew I had arrived just in time. Lunch would start soon, flooding the office with students, and reducing the staff present. Since I arrived before lunch, I walked up to the front desk, and was helped immediately.

"How are you Emily? I haven't seen you in a while." The secretary behind the front desk asked. She was one of those kind women that worked in Elementary Schools because they loved children, and often greeted anyone who walked through the office with a smile. When I was a student here, I remembered thinking she was old, but she was likely not much older than Ally and Sarah. She was definitely younger than my mom, and I felt bad for thinking she was old when I was younger.

Then again, young kids think *everyone* is old. I was shocked Vee hadn't called me old yet. I would probably die if she called me old.

I returned the secretary's smile. This was part of the reason why I had chosen the school to *accidentally* run into Officer Stevens. If she was suspicious of me being here, I had plenty of staff who would vouch for me being here pretty regularly—at least when I'd lived here.

"I'm doing as well as I can, Mrs. Miller." I admitted. "I moved with my sister and her husband to Virginia. After what happened…" I paused, not sure how to finish. "We just needed a fresh start."

Mrs. Miller's smile faded. "I heard about Cole and Analyn. We were all very sad to hear that they died, and in such a tragic way, too. How is your family dealing with it?"

I shook my head. "It's been hard," I breathed, "but we're all dealing with it in our own ways."

She nodded. "Well, what brings you here today? It's a pretty far trip from Virginia."

"I had a break from school," I lied, "And my other sister was making a trip home, so I figured I would join her. But she has a few meetings today, so I figured that instead of sitting around bored, I would come help in Mrs. Jacobs classroom for the afternoon."

"Is Mrs. Jacobs expecting you?" Mrs. Miller asked.

"Yep. I emailed her this morning. She said she would love the help." I answered.

Mrs. Miller smiled. "You always were the best prepared student." She pulled out the binder containing the visitor log. "You know the drill?"

I nodded. "Sure do."

I chose a pen from the cups of pens on the counter and started filling in the fields on the visitor sign-in log. Once I was done, I put the pen back, and handed the binder back to Mrs. Miller. In return, she handed me a bright yellow visitor sticker with my name on it, and the name of the teacher I was visiting.

"Thank you."

"No, thank you," Mrs. Miller replied. "Mrs. Jacobs is lucky to have a student like you want to come help her."

I gave her a tight smile as I placed the sticker on my shirt just below my right shoulder. I knew almost every teacher at the school, because they had either been my teacher, or had taught Cole or Annie. I could have chosen any teacher at this school to volunteer in their classroom today. I chose Mrs. Jacobs because Peter Carlyle was in her class, and his mom was supposed to come in after lunch to volunteer for a few hours.

There was nothing like a little espionage during art time.

13:51 PDT
Chino Hills, California
Hidden Trails Elementary School

TIME IS AN INTERESTING THING. It gives us new memories, while simultaneously muting our previous experiences until they are nothing more than a faint feeling of nostalgia when we return someplace that used to feel like home. Returning to help in Mrs. Jacobs' First Grade classroom somehow felt both super familiar and completely foreign. I could remember core memories from the same age of the students I was helping, and those memories felt like yesterday. But as a seventeen year old preparing to graduate from High School, first grade was more than half my life behind me and felt very far away.

I had most definitely forgotten how chaotic a first grade classroom could be, and had neglected to account for that chaos in making the plan to talk to Officer Stevens. In the shuffle of getting the kids ready for art time, Stevens had ended up on the opposite side of the room from me. My only hope was that I could talk to her before she left.

I started cleaning up the paint sets, carefully stacking them back in the container Mrs. Jacobs kept the paints in while Stevens was helping the students wash their hands at the sink in the back. I looked up as a little boy came running up to me, his excitement running over into the happy way he tapped his feet as he stood next to me, waiting for me to notice. I smiled. "What's up Peter?" I asked the little boy that I knew better than most of the kids in the class.

He looked at me a little surprised since I called him by his actual name instead of his Generation code name *Mercury*. His surprise quickly morphed into suspicion, his eyes narrowing as he looked at me. "Challenge," he said.

My smile widened. With the children in the program being so young, we expanded the usual *stranger danger* teachings. We were asking children, who were notoriously chatty, and trusting, to keep secrets. So we taught them code words. Someone finds out about the Promising Generation, and approaches one of the kids asking questions about the program, they could say *Challenge*. It was simple enough the young kids could remember it, but only someone who was part of the program would know what to respond.

We also taught their parents a select passphrase with their kids. The typical *stranger danger* training taught kids not to go with anyone they didn't recognize. Unfortunately, with their parents' jobs, sometimes they would need to have someone else pick them up. We had the Promising Generation so they could have a network of other CIA parents to call, but if something happened, and they needed to send someone who their kid didn't know, the kids knew they could go with anyone who used the passphrase when they issued their *Challenge.*

I glanced around at the other students, noticing that the only eyes on Peter and I were his mother's, then I squatted down so I was at his eye level. "Camellia. Gold. 2401," I replied. It was my Promising Generation Codename, Level, and PIN.

He squinted his eyes at me, still suspicious. "Passphrase?"

"Zurg is the enemy," I replied. Before the start of school every year, we changed the passphrase. We got the kids involved by letting them choose something to reference, that way it was easy for them to remember. This year, everyone was obsessed with *Toy Story 2*, and the direct to VHS movie *The Adventures of Buzz Lightyear*, so a Zurg reference it was.

Peter nodded, his suspicions about my identity sufficiently defused. "I know you are close with Morningstar," he started, handing me the painting he had just done with the rest of the class. "Can you give this to her?" He asked me.

I stood there gaping at him, and the painting in his hand, unsure how to respond. Mrs. Jacobs had told them to paint something for someone special. Most of the kids had painted something for their parents, or a sibling, or maybe a friend. Taking the paper from him was harder than I thought. The kids that were part of the Promising Generation were a tight knit group. I knew that. But to have him care enough about my niece to give her his art project that he was meant to give to someone special…

"Moving can be hard. You have to make new friends. She was nice to me when I moved here. I want her to know that I won't forget about her." Peter told me, still holding the paper out to me.

"Thank you," I said. "I'm sure this will mean a lot to her."

He nodded, turning and walking away. I stood up, my eyes glued to the painting, and the chicken scratch that represented a first-grader's hand writing at the bottom of the page.

I will miss you, my Mira Nova.

I looked up from the painting, finding Peter sitting back at his desk, waiting for Mrs. Jacobs to start them on their next task.

"His heart is so pure," a voice commented from beside me. I turned toward the voice to see that it belonged to Peter's mother, Officer Elisabeth Stevens.

"Mrs. Stevens," I greeted her. I gestured to the paper. "Your son is very thoughtful. I didn't know he knew her very well."

"Please, call me Elisabeth. And I think that little boy has a crush." She laughed. "He has been asking why she hasn't been at meetings. Every week."

I nodded, my heart twinging the slightest little bit. But I couldn't focus on it. I had a mission to accomplish. "I think she misses it too," I admitted, trying to find some common ground to talk to her. "Just a couple days ago, I had to drag her away from the playground to go home and do homework because she wanted to stay and *train*." I sighed. "I understand why Sarah did it though. It shocked all of us, having the enemy so close, and not having any idea. I can't imagine what all of the parents must be feeling, knowing that their kids might not be safe."

Elisabeth tried to hide a cringe, but I still caught it.

Cole was right. She wasn't willingly helping the Circle of Fifths. She looked over at her son, sitting still in his seat. If the Circle of Fifths was using Peter to control her, though, she might not be willing to help me. Protecting her son would be her priority. And I couldn't promise to keep him safe. I wasn't much more than a child myself, and I didn't even live here any more. I lived in Virginia. With my niece. Keeping her safe. If Peter would always come first for her, Vee always came first for me.

"Mrs. Jacobs doesn't need our help for a little bit, let's go for a walk," Elisabeth suggested.

Something about the suggestion made me nervous, but I nodded anyway. Asking me to go for a walk could be Elisabeth's way of getting me someplace where we could talk freely.

Or it could be her way of getting me alone to eliminate an issue for the Circle of Fifths.

Elisabeth waved at Mrs. Jacobs, who smiled and nodded as she asked the class to return to their seats and settle down. Once we were out of the classroom, Elisabeth looked at me.

"I take it Cole is alive," she said nonchalantly.

I didn't let her words shake my control. "Cole died in the explosion." I replied.

Elisabeth shook her head. "Cole wasn't in the house when it

exploded. But you're here, meaning Cole must have found someone in the family. Probably Ally. He's safe." She explained, but not to convince me. She wasn't addressing me. It was like she was talking to herself. "He told her that I pulled him out, which is why you have sought me out."

Elisabeth shocked me, when out of nowhere, she turned to me and enveloped me in a hug.

"I'm so sorry I couldn't save Analyn. I tried. I really tried," she mumbled. She pulled out from the hug. "I want to help you take down the Circle of Fifths. I've never agreed with their mission, but any group that is willing to kill kids to achieve their mission is too evil to be allowed to exist."

I shook my head, trying to ward off the surprise I felt from her statement. "I can't offer you anything."

"Yes you can." Elisabeth told me. "I assume you would like to remove the Circle of Fifths from the Promising Generation."

I nodded.

Elisabeth smiled. "That's what you can offer me. Remove the Circle of Fifths from the Promising Generation. Peter is my world, but he isn't safe as long as the Circle of Fifths has access. So what do you need from me?"

"Confirmation on who is Circle of Fifths," I answered. "I identified two kids who each have at least one parent who is Circle of Fifths. Peter is one of them. Is it just you, or is it your husband as well?"

"I'm not married," Elisabeth said. "Peter's father and I never got married. We—It's complicated, but the gist of it is that I didn't plan for Peter to happen, but when I found out I was pregnant, I knew I wanted to keep him, and I thought his father should be in his life. That was a mistake. I had already applied to join Sarah's group, so as soon as he found out, he thought using me and Peter to get onto Sarah's team would help him increase his use in the Circle of Fifths. He was right." Elisabeth took a deep breath. "Look, I know that even if he doesn't figure out that I am helping you, he's not going to let me continue to have a relationship with Peter. I am being transferred."

"Does Peter know?" I asked.

Elisabeth shook her head. "I'm not allowed to tell him. There is only one other parent who is Circle of Fifths," she said, redirecting the conversation. "Kyrie Jackson McKenzie. Her husband isn't involved, and keeping her involvement from him is stressful for her. I think I have been slowly shifting her allegiance away from the Circle of Fifths. It's been hard, because she's a legacy, so turning against the Circle, is turning her back on her family."

"And you think she will turn against her family?" I asked. With Elisabeth leaving, having another asset inside the Circle of Fifths might be useful. The problem was, turning an asset against their own family was always hard, and never recommended. Unless it was against a distant or abusive relative, their loyalties would always be divided, and it was impossible to ensure they sided with you.

"I don't know a mother who wouldn't give everything to provide what's best for her child." Elisabeth answered, "Kyrie is no different. The Circle of Fifths doesn't care about its agents. She wants a way out. Not just for herself, but for her son."

I took a deep breath, then nodded. "Before I meet with her, I need you to make sure."

She nodded. "Kalen and Peter have a playdate after school. I'll talk to her when she picks Kalen up. Assuming she agrees, how would you like me to contact you?"

"I'll give you my cell number when we get back to the classroom." I told her. "What time should I expect to hear from you?"

"She's picking Kalen up at six, so around then." Elisabeth told me.

I nodded, letting her lead me back to the classroom.

17:49 PDT
Chino Hills, California
Faultline

WATCHING MICHAEL AND ALLY INTERACT at dinner was both adorable and nauseating. You would think that I was used to seeing my older siblings happily married and in love. After all, they all were, and I had lived with Sarah and Neil for years.

I was probably just jealous.

I wasn't naive. I knew that my siblings' marriages weren't perfect. I could see the strain Sarah and Neil's marriage was under, and if I was completely honest with myself, I wasn't sure if they would make it, as much as we all wanted them to. Dylan's job kept him away from Addy and their young family all too often. Michael and Ally? They had spent years trying to make a long distance relationship work, and now that they were married and didn't have that distance as an obstacle, they had an entirely new set of issues to work through.

I didn't envy any of them. And yet—

The small metallic chime of my Timex broke my thoughts. I turned it off, pushing my chair back.

"Where are you headed?" Ally asked. It was as if the scraping of my chair legs against the tile reminded her of my presence, and she suddenly had to pretend to care.

That was mean. Apparently my thoughts were extremely bitter, even though it was *my* decision not to date anyone at the moment. I didn't need the distraction. Vee needed my attention—when I was done making sure she was safe, that was.

My goodness, I was starting to sound like my older sisters. I was making excuses for my absence by saying it was for someone's safety. Yuck.

"I'm expecting a phone call." I answered simply, pushing my chair back in.

Michael glanced at Ally, leaning over to give her a gentle kiss on her forehead. "Come back safe," he told her. His voice was soft, a quiet plead to his wife as an answer to her unasked question.

She wanted to come with me.

"You are my home." Ally's response sounded like the line from a romance movie, but I'd missed the rest of the movie, so I didn't understand the context. Their interaction felt natural, hinting at the years of conversations they'd had previously. I may have been Ally's sister, but I was no longer one of the few people in the world who knew her the way only her closest family would. Michael was her closest family now, and I didn't know her even *remotely* as well as Michael did.

I walked away, leaving before I saw any more of their private moment. I had to fight my annoyance over the situation. They acted as if they were the only two who needed to be consulted over the decision for Ally to come with me. Why not ask me? It was my phone call. It was my meeting. It was my mission.

But I knew having Ally to support me was smart. No matter how I spun it, I was still a minor. I was a not-quite-an-adult-aged-spy who could make promises, but didn't have an agency to support me and give validity to my promises, because I wasn't old enough to officially join one.

Ally had the authority to make promises that would be supported by multiple agencies. Having her come with me would add authenticity to our agreement.

I was expecting Ally to try to take control. I expected her to take the keys, and decide where to go to get the cell signal I would need to receive the call.

Instead, she climbed into the passenger seat, and asked, "What's the plan?"

19:14 PDT
Chino Hills, California
Stevens House

SURPRISINGLY, MY PLAN WAS WORKING better than I had even hoped. We had been within cell range when Elisabeth called, telling Ally and I that Kyrie wanted to help.

Now, Ally, Elisabeth, and Kyrie were discussing the protections Ally could provide for them and their boys if they fed us information about the Circle of Fifths, while I helped Kalen and Peter with homework. They had offered to have me join them, but I knew Elisabeth and Kyrie were both helping us because they cared about their children. I figured a good way of showing them I did too, was choosing to watch them, instead of sit in on a meeting I had been essential in setting up. It would be a great first step for launching my career with the agency. But I hadn't set up the meeting hoping it would give me a leg up when I joined the CIA.

My future career was not as important as protecting my niece and the other kids in the Promising Generation.

"Camellia, what are our mom's talking to Aphrodite about?" Kalen asked me.

"That's not Aphrodite." Peter corrected Kalen. "It just looks like Aphrodite, but it's not her."

I had to fight a smile, knowing that even Peter could tell my older sisters apart. Ally would be so mad if she found out, and she would, because there was no way I was going to miss an opportunity to tell her that she and Sarah weren't as interchangeable as they once thought they were.

"Are we at Headquarters?" I asked the two boys.

"No," they replied in unison.

"Then what are the rules for talking about people we know from the program?" I followed up.

"Use their name," the boys replied.

"Kalen, do you want to try to ask your question again?" I asked him.

He nodded. "Emily, what are our moms talking to the girl who looks like Sarah about?"

"Much better, thank you Kalen," I replied. "And I don't know what they're talking about, because the conversation is Top Secret. Do you remember what we do when something Top Secret happens?" I asked them.

Something I had learned working with the Promising Generation, was that every moment was a teaching moment, and using real world happenings to help them learn what we were teaching in the Promising Generation was extremely useful. I may feel a little bad about not telling Peter and Kalen what their moms were discussing with Ally, but the fewer people who knew, the better.

And that included the kids.

"We don't tell anyone," Peter answered.

I nodded. "That's right. We don't tell anyone that the meeting even happened. That includes your dads." I looked at both boys to make sure they understood. I wasn't really concerned about Kalen's dad, since Elisabeth had told me that Kyrie was the only one of Kalen's parents who worked for the Circle of Fifths, but I didn't want to single out Peter, and make the boys nervous about what was happening. I wanted to stress the importance of not sharing that the meeting happened, but not terrify them.

We might not trust Peter's dad, but at the end of the day, he was still Peter's dad, and he would soon be Peter's only parent. Besides that, George might get suspicious if Peter suddenly started acting twitchy around him. We needed to make sure George didn't suspect anything was wrong for as long as possible.

Peter gave me a short little nod that he had probably learned from his father. I was sure when his dad did it, he looked like the well-trained agent he was. The same nod on Peter looked almost comical. That was the one down side of training these kids to be spies, starting so young. In a way, I almost felt like we were asking them to grow up way too fast. I had seen it happening with Cole. He was always protective of his younger sisters, but giving him the training we had put that pressure on his shoulders more than it had already been. I couldn't help but wonder if he still would have run to London if we hadn't trained him. He could have been home, with his parents and surviving sisters. He could have been at home, grieving Analyn's death with us, not trying to work through that by himself, in another country.

If I had anything to say about it, I would do everything I could to make sure the Circle of Fifths didn't succeed in robbing these boys of their childhood.

19:32 PDT
Chino Hills, California
Stevens House

THE SECOND THE CAR DOORS closed, Ally let out a massive sigh.

"Do I dare ask how it went?" I asked as I started the car.

"It went better than I had hope for when I talked to you in DC," Ally admitted. "I thought we would identify the mole, and then talk to Deputy Director McLean about trying to remove them. I hadn't even thought about flipping them. When you told me there was more than one, and that you wanted to turn one…"

"You had your doubts," I finished.

"I had my concerns," Ally corrected. "I learned a long time ago to never doubt you." She took a deep breath before continuing. "And you just proved yourself even more today. Not only did you turn one agent, you turned two. They trust you, Emily. I was able to arrange some protections for them, but they both told me that they would be completely comfortable having you be their handler."

My brain started to panic, considering all the ways this could go horribly wrong for me, or worse, for Kyrie and Elisabeth and their kids. I took a couple of deep breaths, watching the road as I was driving; I needed to ground myself to prevent an anxiety attack. If I had an anxiety attack right now, I could harm *way* too many people.

A couple of months ago, this would have been all I wanted. Being given the chance to turn and handle two assets in the Circle of Fifths was the opportunity of a lifetime, and I was only 17. I was *barely* 17. Kind of. I guess technically my half birthday had just passed, and I was getting closer to 18 everyday. I was supposed to be making progress, not regressing. Even yesterday when Ally asked me to come with her, I argued my strengths. Mere hours ago, I was convincing Ally that I knew what I was doing, and could turn an asset. But now that I had proved myself, I was questioning my abilities. My insecurities were winning. And I knew where they were coming from—how could I protect Peter and Kalen when I couldn't even help protect my own nieces and nephew?

"What do I have to do?" I asked. "What did you promise them?"

I could feel Ally's eyes on my as I took my deep breaths, using blurred white lines of the road as a visual anchor to keep me in the moment. "You are ready for this." Ally reassured. "As for what I promised them, they just want their boys to be safe. When we get back to the safehouse, I am going to use the secure line to call Deputy Director McLean. We need to arrange to have George Carlyle transferred. Elisabeth's transfer is already pending. That will just leave Kyrie in the Promising Generation. She will report to you what the Circle of Fifths is asking for, or having her do, and she will ask you what bent truths she should give them. When their intel helps take down the Circle of Fifths, they get out, and their boys never have to join."

"How am I supposed to handle them when I am living in Virginia" I asked, realizing that besides my own insecurities, not being near the assets I am handling will be extremely difficult.

"You will have to figure that out with Kyrie and Elisabeth," Ally answered.

"When are you taking me home?" I asked Ally, trying to make an itinerary for the rest of my stay in California. I already had some ideas running through my head for how I could best handle my two assets, but I thought it would be best if I met with them in person to discuss them.

It would probably be best to communicate with Kyrie and Elisabeth via burner phones. Emails could be hacked, and it would be timely and difficult to come up with a code we could use. Emails also had the added drawback of being able to trace it to the user. Burner phones could be bought with cash, and you could buy minutes as necessary and pay for those with cash as well. That way if the Circle of Fifths ever got suspicious of Elisabeth or Kyrie and ever put their phones under surveillance, there wouldn't be anything betraying their extracurricular activities. We would create a set schedule for when they needed to call in and report, and create a simple text message code that we could use if they needed help, or got burned.

There was so much for me to plan, and fail safes to put in place… I didn't want anything to happen to Elisabeth, Peter, Kyrie, Jason, or Kalen. Not if I could help it.

"We leave tomorrow morning." Ally replied.

In other words, I had a lot to do, and no time to do it. This was going to be great.

20:16 PDT
Chino Hills, California
Hall Home

Hades is in danger. Zurg is coming.

I read the text message I'd received from an unknown number another time. The *Zurg* reference told me it was someone in the Promising Generation, since they knew that *Zurg* was part of this year's code phrase, and *Hades* was Kalen's codename. But Kalen didn't have a phone. Or my phone number.

Someone did. And they wanted me to know that he was in trouble. The Circle of Fifths was coming for him.

The timing was suspicious. It had been less than two hours since Kyrie agreed to help us, and already the Circle of Fifths was coming for her son? Either it was a trap, and Kyrie had never meant to help us, or Kyrie was being surveilled by the Circle of Fifths, and they knew she was betraying them.

I dialed the phone number that texted me. It had barely started ringing when the line connected.

"My house was bugged," Kyrie said as she answered the phone. "Those bastards took me expressing my concerns as disloyalty. I wouldn't be surprised if my own brother was sent in to place the bugs."

This was bad. Very bad. Kyrie was supposed to stay in the Promising Generation and help us feed the Circle of Fifths bad intel, but protecting Kyrie, Jason, and Kalen was the priority. If the house was bugged, that meant that she couldn't stay and play double agent. They already had their suspicions. Any information she gave them would be subjected to extra scrutiny. We would *have* to give them *completely* factual information, and I couldn't do that in good conscious. I couldn't risk the lives and safety of the children in the Promising Generation to solidify Kyrie's cover. But if I couldn't solidify her cover, I couldn't leave her with them. We had to pull her out.

The sooner the better.

"Where are you right now?"

"I went for a walk," Kyrie answered. "I knew that I needed to reach out and let you know that I wouldn't be able to help you the way I promised Ally. I'm sorry. I can't contact you again."

"Don't hang up," I said. "It doesn't matter if you can help us or not. You were willing to ruin your relationship with your family in order to help us. We promised to protect you and your family. You want out. I will need to arrange for a safehouse, but…go home, get packed. I'll be there within an hour, and I will get you out."

"Emily… I can't ask that of you." Kyrie said. "I can't help you take down the Circle of Fifths. I can't help protect the other kids."

"Removing the Circle of Fifths influence and participation in the Promising Generation will help us protect those kids more than you can even know. And you have helped with that. If you want out from the Circle of Fifths, we can fake your deaths, get you new identities, and move you someplace they won't find you."

"Thank you," Kyrie said on the other side of the phone. "I will grab our go-bags, and get Kalen ready to leave." I listened as Kyrie sighed on the other side of the phone. "Any suggestions on how I can convince Jason to leave? It's not like I can come clean. Not with the house bugged."

"I don't know," I admitted.

Kyrie laughed. "Didn't think so, but I had to ask."

"Good luck." I said, before she hung up.

I moved my plan for handling Elisabeth and Kyrie to the side. I had an extraction plan to come up with instead.

20:24 PDT
Chino Hills, California
Faultline

"HOW LONG WOULD IT TAKE to get Waterfall ready to use?" I asked Ally as I walked into the living room of Faultline. I hated disturbing her. She looked so comfortable. Her head was in Michael's lap, where he was playing with her hair while she read a book.

Ally looked up at me, a look of confusion on her face. "Why do you need to use Waterfall? If you want to stay a little longer you can just stay here. I don't think mom has gotten around to selling her house yet either. I know it isn't as safe as this one, and it probably has too many memories of Annie…"

"It's not for me," I said. "But I might need to stay. For I don't know how long."

Ally closed her book, sitting up. "Who was burned?"

"Kyrie," I replied. "She just found some bugs in her house."

Ally set her book on the coffee table. "So you need an extraction plan, and you haven't had time to come up with one yet…" Ally guessed. "Waterfall would need some food and other basic supplies, but it's also a long drive to the staging house."

"Yeah, but Waterfall is the safest of safehouses." I pointed at Michael. "I mean look at him. He's still alive."

Ally sighed. "Waterfall is definitely the hardest to get to, and is our family's favorite safehouse, but it would probably be best to use a closer safehouse. What is your extraction plan?"

"Pick them up from their house and get them to a safehouse. Once I have them somewhere safe, I can plan from there." I replied.

Ally stood up and grabbed some keys.

"What are you doing?" I asked.

"You don't have a real plan, you don't know where all of the safehouses are, and you are going to need help. You've got heart Emily. Let me help you." Ally stated.

I sighed. She was right. I asked about Waterfall, because besides this safehouse, I didn't know where the other California safehouses were. I knew Waterfall because I had spent some time there with Ally, Michael, and Rafael when the Circle of Fifths was threatening Michael and Rafael to get their father, Lord Thomas Feilds, to cave to their demands. After the house explosion that Vee survived, the Circle of Fifths had started making attempts to eliminate the remaining survivor, no matter the collateral damage. After they caused me to wreck my Suzuki, we spent a week at Faultline before we moved to Waterfall.

"Take a couple of our security team with you," Michael told Ally, grabbing her hand to make sure she paused to listen to him before running out the door with me.

"Michael..."

"No. You're going because you are concerned about the Circle of Fifths showing up and Emily not being able to protect herself," Michael said firmly. I don't think I had ever heard him be firm with Ally. He and Ally were partners, never making demands of each other, rather discussing anything of importance, so they were both able to express their concerns. His tone made me listen to him, and I could tell it made Ally listen too. "It's dangerous. We have Kate at home. You promised you wouldn't take any unnecessary risks. That means taking security."

"Fine," Ally conceded. I could tell she didn't want to. She wanted to fight. But Michael had used her daughter. Ally needed to be careful, because she had a little girl at home that needed her mum.

I turned my back to my sister and her husband, closing my eyes, and taking some deep breaths. I had let myself get carried away. I was so concerned about protecting Cole and Vee that I had blindly followed my sister to California. I had let myself believe that I could count on her to follow me anywhere to protect the children of our family and the Promising Generation. But there was one very big difference between Ally and I, and it wasn't our age. I would do absolutely anything to protect Cole, Alyx, Thane, Chelsi, Kate, and Cassie. I would risk my life to save the children of the Promising Generation, and I would gladly give my life if it meant keeping my nieces and nephews safe. I knew Ally, Sarah, Dylan, Michael, Addy, and Neil would all do the same, but at the end of the day, they had to remember that their children needed them in their lives too.

If I died, my death would be sad, and my nieces and nephews might miss me for a while, but they would still have a fairly normal upbringing. If one of my siblings or their spouses died, their children would grow up without a parent.

I knew what it was like to lose a parent. All of my siblings were adults when our dad died. They were married. Cole, Analyn, Thane, and Alyx had all been born.

I was twelve. I had been at home to watch mom mourn—or avoid mourning, as the case had been. I knew I wasn't the only one who felt his lost, but I felt alone in it. Mom withdrew, and eventually took off, deciding it was too painful to stay in California where dad had grown up. I got left behind. Ally, Sarah, and Dylan all relied on their spouses to support them through dad's loss. I lost both parents.

When Sarah and Neil moved into Mom and Dad's house to take care of me, I had been moody, and quiet. I was angry at everyone. I was angry at dad for dying. I was angry at mom for leaving. I was angry at Sarah and Neil for trying to replace them. I was angry at Ally for having the chance to have dad walk her down the aisle.

But I was old enough to remember my dad, and understand what was going on.

I couldn't let one of my siblings die. I couldn't put one of my nieces or nephews through what I had been through. They had been my salvation when I was headed down a path of self-destruction.

With shoulders rolled back, I made a mental list of my objectives heading into enemy territory: Save the child, protect my asset…

And keep my sister alive at all costs.

21:06 PDT
Chino Hills, California
McKenzie House

"EMILY, YOU STAY IN THE car," Ally ordered as Chevy Suburban her security team was renting stopped in front of the McKenzie house.

"Absolutely not." I argued. "This is my asset. My mission. My operation. My extraction."

"We need someone in the car, so if things get dicey and we need to make a quick get-away, we can," Ally stated, taking her seatbelt off.

I pointed at the MI:6 agent from her detail that had driven the SUV to this house in the first place. "He's already in the drivers seat. I don't need to stay behind as well."

"Michael insisted I bring them, but if we have access to two well trained agents, I'm going to use them." Ally told me. "Lewis, Wood. Perimeter sweep. Lewis leave the keys."

The two agents got out of the front seat, the driver leaving the keys behind. I looked at Ally, trying desperately to take deep breaths to maybe prevent my frustration from turning into anger. "I can do a perimeter sweep just as well as either of those two agents." I argued. "I'm not some subordinate you can just order around. I'm your sister. I am *extremely* capable, as you pointed hour mere hours ago. Stop trying to sideline me."

"I know you are capable. I know you can do a perimeter sweep. I know you can probably even talk the asset inside out of the house with ease. But you don't have experience deescalating angry spouses who just discovered their partner has been lying to them for the entirety of their relationship. I do. That's why I am going in. And not to criticize my security team, but they can't drive as well as you. Not on the right side of the road. That's why I need you driving."

"And it's just convenient that the car is the safest place," I said

"Emily, don't."

"Sorry, but I'm going to. Michael is right. You need to be safe. You have a toddler at home that needs her mom. I have no one that counts on me. This was my idea. This is my fault. If anyone should be putting themselves in danger, it should be me," I argued.

Ally looked out the window as Wood gave her a small nod, indicating that their perimeter sweep came back clean. The house was safe—for now. The longer we stayed here arguing, the higher probability that we wouldn't be. "This argument isn't over," Ally said, looking out the window. She glanced back at me. "You might not be a mother yet, but you are very important to many kids lives."

Ally opened the door, getting out of the Suburban and closing the door and any chance I had to argue against her.

I hated when she did that.

Ally walked up to the front door, and knocked. It didn't take very long for Kyrie to open the door and let Ally in. Lewis and Wood began a rotation, ensuring they had all the possible entrances covered, so the house remained secure as long as Ally was inside. I was still annoyed, and I would definitely continue this argument with Ally once everyone was safely in the Suburban and we were driving to a safehouse, but I wasn't going to do anything to jeopardize everyone's lives by getting out of the Suburban and making it so we couldn't make a quick get-away. With a dramatic eye roll no one would see, I hopped over the seats, sliding into the dark cloth driver's seat.

Once I was settled in the driver's seat with my seatbelt buckled, I checked my mirrors, adjusting the rear and side view mirrors. It didn't matter that I wasn't driving yet. Adjusting them now meant I wouldn't waste precious time later adjusting them if we needed to get away. Having them properly adjusted now also meant I could be a look-out while I was at it, with a 360 degree view of the street.

With Lewis and Wood checking the back yard, and all the entry points on the house, it was best if I used my vantage point on the street to remain alert to suspicious cars that circled more than once, or shadowy figures that tried to use the neighbor houses as cover to move in and strike. My eyes began a rotation of their own, checking out the windshield, the rear view mirror, the driver's side mirror, the driver's side window, the passenger side window, the passenger side mirror, and back around again.

As the minutes droned on, thankfully, nothing exciting happened. The problem was, I needed to remain alert, and not become lax in my checks of the street. In a way, what I was doing was similar to what cops did when they were staking out a house or a business. I had watched more than a few cop shows with my parents when I was little, and the habit had continued after my dad had died, and I was living with Sarah and Neil. Every Sunday, we sat down and watched Midsommer Murders, or another one of the British Series. I had also become obsessed with watching Law and Order, and when CSI had started, I watched that one too. The problem with watching those, however, is it always gave me anxiety when they had a stake-out scene. The two partners sat in the car, chatting away, sometimes even going so far as to look at their partner they were talking to. As I watched those scenes, I always held my breath, waiting for them to miss the person they were looking for walking into the building they were watching, because they were more engaged in the conversation, rather than their job.

I couldn't let myself lose focus. Instead of losing the bad guy I was looking for if I missed something, I could be risking the lives of everyone inside. If Ally was going to put me in the car, I was going to make sure she stayed safe inside, regardless as to whether or not I agreed with her decision. The best way I could think of to keep my focus was make it into a game, or just something fun.

"North Sector, all clear," I said out loud using a low, fake radio voice as I checked out the windshield.

I made a nasally voice as I checked the driver's side mirror and window, saying "East Sector, all clear."

"We got nothing in the West," I said using my normal voice as I checked the passenger side mirror and window."

"South sector, all clear."

I made the rotation several more times, allowing myself to use a fun voice after I had checked each side.

"Still got nothing in the Ea—" I stopped my game as I saw movement in the driver's mirror. Because it was so late, it was hard to see, but a shadow was moving across the street at the closest intersection. I watched, waiting to see if the figure stuck to the sidewalks, or if they clung to the shadows. I followed their movement from the driver's side mirror, to the rearview mirror, and finally to the passenger side mirror as they crossed the street.

Once the person got across the street, they ran up to the front of a house, and began using the darkness around the bushes and foliage in front of houses to blend into the night. The only reason I could see them was because I had caught the movement when they ran across the street, and was tracking them from there.

It was time to go.

I turned the key in the ignition, the 5.3 Liter V-8 engine of the Chevrolet Surbuban 1500 roaring to life. Lewis, who was currently walking across the front of the house, heard the car and looked over at me. I turned the lights on, and put the automatic transmission in reverse, using the reverse lights to light up the figure creeping through bushes. He nodded at me, running for the front door. I kept my eye on the figure, watching as it got closer and closer.

To my relief, the front door opened quickly, and people immediately started filing out. I watched with baited breath as Kyrie came out the door carrying Kalen. The next person out the door was Kyrie's husband, Jason. Ally, ever the protector, brought up the rear.

Despite Kyrie being the most likely target of an attack, Lewis put his hand on Ally's back, following closely to her. I knew she likely hated it, more than she would ever admit, but she was his protectee, and he was going to do his job. Personally, I was grateful for him.

Wood had reappeared, and ran ahead of the others, opening the back passenger side door for the group of people coming towards the Suburban. He then planted himself behind the door, watching the figure that was now hiding in the next door neighbor bushes.

Why had they stopped moving forward? My silent question was answered as I heard a metallic ding from the back of the Suburban. My eyes shot to the people I had promised to protect, feeling fleeting relief as I saw they were all still running to the car, now slightly faster than they had been.

Ally pulled a Glock from a holster she was hiding underneath her blazer. I wasn't sure how long it had been there. Had she had that gun all day, or had she grabbed it from the safehouse… right now it didn't matter. She had it. And she knew how to use it. With it free of the holster, she held it in her right hand down by her side, as she passed the others to the car, perching next to Wood before returning fire. Kyrie climbed into the car with Kalen shielded in her arms, and climbed straight to the back. Her husband followed her, the two of them sandwiching Kalen in the seat between them.

"Get in the car," Lewis ordered Ally once Jason had gotten in the car.

"You first. I'm providing cover." Ally replied.

Of course Ally would argue. "All of you in. *Now*." I said from the front seat.

Ally glanced at me. I wondered what she saw when she looked at my face. I hoped she could see just how serious I was, and didn't see an insecure, inexperienced, younger sister.

Ally turned back towards the house, sending off two more shots for cover, then jumped in the car. Lewis followed right behind her, slamming the door shut behind him, as Wood opened the front door and climbed in.

Before Wood had shut the passenger door, I had my foot on the gas, squealing the tires as the SUV's tires tried to find traction to match the power being delivered to them from the engine. "Seatbelts!" I hollered. If I was going to have to drive evasively, I wanted to make sure everyone was secure in the car. The last thing we needed was one of the passengers being thrown across the back seat of the Suburban. It would be pointless to save them from injury and death only to cause injury or death with my driving.

21:54 PDT
Chino Hills, California

THE TIRES SQUEALED AS I rounded another right-hand corner at speeds high enough I was terrified the Suburban would roll. I swear the drivers side tires were leaving the road, but as I straightened out the steering wheel, the Suburban righted itself and continued on down the road.

"I think you have better car control than Lewis," Wood commented from the passenger seat. "How old is she again?" He turned around in his seat to ask Ally.

"Focus," Ally criticized. "I think we lost them." She reported. "Fortunately they didn't send an entire team."

"They will," Kyrie said. "Phil will make sure of it."

"I still can't understand. Why does your brother want you dead?" Jason asked.

I tuned out the conversation in the backseat. Everyone else was starting to get comfortable, thinking we were safe for the moment, but I knew that Kyrie was right. Her brother would come for her and everyone who helped Kyrie escape. We may not have been followed by the Circle of Fifths agent, but he saw what we were driving, he put some bullet holes in the passenger rear quarter panel. He was there long enough he probably memorized our plate. He saw which way we went. He didn't need to follow us. He saw the security detail. As much as I appreciated having them to keep Ally safe, if they insisted that we followed their protocols, we would all end up dead.

I needed to make sure that didn't happen.

"What is your protocol," I asked Wood quietly so I wouldn't be heard by Ally over the conversation happening in the back seat.

I could see Wood glancing at Ally sitting behind me before looking back forward. "We are supposed to secure your sister at a secure location until we can ensure the danger has passed."

"There are other members of the security team, correct?"

"Yes," Wood confirmed.

I nodded, glad I was right. "How soon can the team get the plane we flew in on ready."

"Not long, why? I already told you the protocol."

I turned left on the street I knew would take me to the airport, instead of right towards the hotel suite they likely wanted me to take Ally to. "We follow your protocol, the Circle of Fifths will find us, and will kill us all." I told Wood. "We are going to the airport."

"We don't have clearance to bring—"

"Not all of us. You are going to contact Michael and his team, and get them to the airport. Your team will get Michael and Ally on that plane, and take them back to London. Your priority is to keep my sister and her family safe. If I get out of your way, you can do your job, and I have one less person to worry about protecting."

"Emily, I'm not leaving you behind." Ally said quietly from behind my seat. I don't know when she had started listening to my conversation, but I cursed myself for not paying better attention to her. I really didn't want to try to argue with her about this. A clear picture of Ally playing with Kate the last time I had been in London flashed through my head. I needed to ensure Kate would have many more of those moments as she grew up, and that meant sending Ally home now, not keeping her in the United States with me, moving from safehouse to safehouse to protect Kyrie and her family.

"You need to get back to Kate. It doesn't make sense for me to go with you anyway. I can find my own way to DC." I replied.

"You are going to stay with them in the safehouse until you figure out how to keep them safe long term and you know it." Ally chastised. "If you're going to lie, at least make it believable."

"Truth?" I asked.

"That would be preferable." Ally retorted.

"The truth is I am the only one who doesn't have a child depending on me. Truth is I can't ask any of my nieces or nephews to go through what I did when dad died. And the unfortunate truth of you running into that house instead of me is that now *your* voice is on the tapes of Kyrie betraying her brother. Now *your* name is on the Circle of Fifths hit list. This is my fault, and I can't let you die because I wanted it all. I can't let Kate grow up without a mom because I thought *I* could be the one to take down the Circle of Fifths. I can't let you die because I made the same mistake dad did."

When I finished my rant, the car was dead silent. Even the lover's quarrel in the back seat had been silenced by my admission.

Great. Just what I wanted. Pity.

"I am taking you to the airport so your husband will drag you home. If you and Sarah can't be inherently good mothers, at least your husbands can encourage you to be." I added. "You should be a mother. I will be a spy."

I kept waiting for someone to say something. I kept waiting for a whisper or a sigh. I couldn't even hear a single breath. It was like everyone was afraid to breathe.

Kalen didn't even make a noise.

After some of the tension in the air dissipated, Wood pulled out a phone and dialed a number.

"It's Wood. Champion is compromised. Proceed with Adventurer's extraction plan. Urgent."

The phone call was short and sweet, but I knew the message had been communicated, and once it was over, the car returned to silence. I took a deep breath and let the silence allow me to think, instead of fidgeting in discomfort.

Awkwardness was a mindset. If I didn't think it was awkward to argue with my sister in front of an audience, it wouldn't feel awkward. If I didn't think about it, and let my thoughts obsess over everything that had been said... Instead, I tried to think about everything I needed to do.

First, I needed to get Ally and Michael out of the United States.

Second, I needed to get Kyrie, Jason, and Kalen to a safehouse.

Third, I needed to fake their death. If they were dead, no one would look for them. It would have been possible to hide them for the rest of their lives, but they would always have to look over their shoulder, and they would have to move constantly. If I faked their deaths, and gave them new identities, they could settle down and live a decent life.

My eyes flicked around my mirrors, just like they had while I was acting as a look-out at the McKenzie house. It didn't matter that I was pretty sure we had lost our tail. I needed to stay vigilant to make sure they didn't come back.

I drove around in a giant circle for over an hour, to make sure we didn't have a tail. Once I knew I had given Michael's team enough time to get to the airport, and there had been enough time given to the pilots to get the plane ready, I headed to the airport.

It was time to check the first thing off of my check-list.

TOP SECRET PROMISING GENERATION EYES ONLY

Operation Subversion
Objective: Systematically dismantle the Circle of Fifths

FIELD REPORT:20 October 2000

CLASSIFIED TOP SECRET

00:01 PDT LAX; Los Angeles, CA
04:25 PDT Terrible's; Jean, NV
04:37 PDT LAX; Los Angeles, CA
05:02 PDT Lamb Park; Las Vegas, NV
05:25 PDT CoF So Cal Station; Los Angeles, CA
10:45 PDT Lamb Park; Las Vegas, NV

00:01 PDT
Los Angeles, California
LAX

THE PLANE WAS WAITING ON the tarmac when we arrived at the airport. Before the car had even come to a complete stop, Wood and Lewis opened their doors and jumped out. Lewis ran over to Ally's door, opened it for her, and ushered her out.

She was safe. At least she would be.

I parked the car and climbed out. Before I could take Kyrie and her family to a safehouse, I needed a new car. Not only was this one running low on gas from the aimless driving I had done to ensure we didn't have a tail, but we also needed a car without bullet holes.

And a car that hadn't been seen at Kyrie's house.

I was thinking something small, but not so small it wouldn't fit Kyrie's family. It also needed to have surprising speed. Or more importantly, acceleration, to put distance between us and anyone who might chase us, and enough speed to keep that distance.

The problem was, I wasn't old enough to rent a car, and if I had Kyrie or Jason rent the car for us, their name would be on the agreement, and it would be easier to find us.

I was distracted from my thoughts as my maroon 1997 Mitsubishi Mirage pulled up, followed by another black SUV. I watched as Michael climbed out of the drivers door of my Mitsubishi, walking to me to hand me my key.

My eyes went from the key to Michael. "How did you know?" I asked quietly.

Michael smiled. "I know my wife," he said, glancing towards where she was leaned into the SUV where Kyrie and her family were still waiting. "I'm surprised she is leaving with me, but I figured there was no way you were leaving the family you guys went to rescue."

"And you know more about spy things than you let on." I finished for him.

Michael smirked. "You don't think your sister would have married me if I wasn't intelligent enough to call her out, do you? I drew her interest because I could keep up with her, and didn't let her walk all over me."

"And you somehow kept her interest through a long distance relationship that lasted what, five years?"

"Something like that," Michael answered. "Be careful Em." He glanced at Ally again. "I know Ally already asked you to be careful, and she will do that everyday, but I want you to promise me you'll be safe. I always wanted to have a little sister, and while my parents never had a girl, you feel like that little sister. I don't think I would handle losing you very well, and I know Sarah, Ally, and Dylan wouldn't handle it well either."

"I will do my best," I told him. "You already helped me more than you possibly know by bringing me my car."

"I think we already established… I know exactly how much changing cars will help you stay safe. To be absolutely safe, you should change cars at least once more before you arrive at whatever safehouse you are going to next."

I nodded, already trying to figure out where the best place to do that would be.

One of the members of Michael's security team placed a hand on his back, ushering him towards the plane. The Pilots must have finished up their preliminary checklists, because the plane engines started up. They were likely finishing up their final checks. It was time for them to leave.

Ally spun away from Lewis, who was also trying to usher Ally towards the plane, and she came to me. I rolled my eyes.

"Be careful, I know. Michael already told me." I had to raise my voice to ensure my voice was heard over the jet engines on the plane nearby.

Ally kept charging towards me, trapping me in a nearly suffocating hug. "Don't take any more risks than you have to. This isn't your fault. I wish you would have talked to me about Dad sooner."

I had to swallow the tears that were threatening to fall with Ally's words. How could I have explained to Ally and Sarah that my grief was different than what they were going through when dad died? How was I supposed to ask for help when everyone was struggling?

How was I supposed to realize what I was actually feeling when I internalized it all?

I was twelve. What twelve year old is in touch enough with their emotions to vocalize how they are actually feeling?

"What safehouse are you taking them to?" Ally asked, still crushing me her hug. She probably figured her security team was less likely to pull her away from a hug, than a conversation.

"I don't know," I admitted. "We already established I don't have the encyclopedic knowledge of Hall safehouses you do."

"Take them to Lamb Park," Ally told me.

"Where is Lamb Park?" I asked.

"Vegas. It's far enough from here that as long as you're not followed, it will take them a while to find you, but close enough and accessible enough you should be able to get there. Just don't stay for more than a day, or maybe two. Max."

I nodded. "Hopefully once I'm there, I should have time to come up with a plan."

"Do you know where you're going?"

"Yeah. Sarah took me with her to get it ready for an asset a couple years ago. I didn't realize it was one of ours." I admitted.

"Sarah took over Safehouse acquisition and maintenance when mom left." After she told me why Sarah had set up the safehouse, she paused. *Sarah had taken over raising me too when mom left.* "There should be a landline. Call me when you get there," Ally added.

"Champion, it's time to go," Lewis said, gently grabbing Ally's arm.

"I love you Em," she told me one last time before letting go and letting Lewis drag her toward the plane.

"I love you too." I replied, waving to her as she climbed on board the plane. Once Lewis had gotten Ally up the stairs of the small jet, and they disappeared from sight into the plane, one of the flight attendants pulled the stairs up, sealing the door shut.

In eleven hours, Ally would be safely back in Feilds Palace, hugging Kate. That thought alone gave me the motivation to keep going. It was a five hour drive to Vegas, and I would be nearing the 24 hour mark of being awake by the time we got there. There wasn't any time to indulge in the luxury of a nap. I needed to get the McKenzie family on the road to Vegas as soon as possible, which meant I had no idea when I would next be able to sleep.

This was one of the rare occasions that the caffeine of coffee was tempting. I didn't drink coffee, and if I made an exception this time, I knew I would be more likely to make an exception next time things were less dire, and the next thing I would know, I would be drinking coffee in the morning because I couldn't operate without it.

I was prone to addiction after all. My grandparents were proof of that. Correction. My lack of grandparents was proof of that.

With that sobering thought stopping my desire for coffee, I leaned into the Suburban, looking at the family counting on me to keep them safe. "It's time to go." I told them. "We're changing cars."

My message delivered, I walked towards my car. I loved my Mitsubishi Mirage. I hated leaving it behind when I followed Sarah and Neil to Washington. The BMW that Neil's parents gave me to drive Vee and I to school may have been newer and nicer, but my Mitsubishi was the little car that could. It got decent gas milage, but still moved when I asked it to. With the right driver, it had better acceleration than other cars on the road.

I opened the driver's door, looking at how far back the seat was. Standing next to Michael, I didn't feel like he was much taller than me, but this was proof he wasn't as scrawny as I always thought he was. When he stood next to my dad or Dylan, he may have seemed smaller, but he was still plenty tall, and had his own kind of strength.

Jason came up behind me, taking the keys from my hand while I stood there, staring at the driver's seat of my car. "You're exhausted." He told me. "You should take a break. Let someone else drive for a bit."

I opened my mouth to protest, but closed it. Kyrie was already in the passenger seat, and Kalen was buckled in the middle of the back seat. *How long had I zoned out, starting at the driver's seat?*

"Take a nap in the back seat. Jason and I can stay awake long enough to get us out of town. I'm guessing we're heading east." Kyrie told me.

I nodded. "That was the plan."

"Good. We'll wake you up when we stop at a rest stop." Jason promised.

Jason opened the back door for me, waiting until I got settled in to hand me a pillow they must have grabbed from their house before they left.

Before I knew it, all of the doors were shut, and Jason started the car. As soon as the car started moving, the gentle rocking of the suspension as the car went over bumps paired with the noise of the engine lulled me to sleep.

04:25 PDT
Jean, Nevada
Terrible's

MY EYES SHOT OPEN, AS a felt a jolt. I looked around, trying to gain my bearings. When I looked over at the little boy in the seat next to me, I remembered. We were heading to Lamb Park.

The light coming in from outside the windows was too bright. I was only going to sleep for a little bit. But the sky was lightening like it did in the hour or so before sunrise. I checked my watch.

Four hours. I had been asleep for four hours.

Why did it both feel like it wasn't nearly enough, and far too long?

I unbuckled my seatbelt, climbing out of the car only to be immediately hit by the smell of gasoline. I looked around, finding Kyrie using the concrete step the gas pump sat on to stretch, and Jason walking back from the small convenience store in the same parking lot.

"I thought you guys were going to wake me up once we got out of the LA basin." I commented once Jason was back within hearing range.

Jason shrugged, pulling the fuel nozzle from the gas pump before putting it in the car. "You were tired," Jason said. "It didn't seem right to wake you up when I could just as easily keep driving." He selected the regular grade of gas, then pulled the lever on the pump, starting to fill up the car.

"You don't know where we're going," I argued. "How did you pay for gas?" I asked. My head was running a million miles a minute. If he'd used a card to pay for gas, then Kyrie's brother would have a way to find us. "And where are we at?"

"We're just outside Vegas." Kyrie told me. "We just drove straight through."

"I used cash," Jason told me. "That's why I went inside."

I took a deep breath. I didn't have to try and figure out where another safehouse was. If Jason had used a card so close to where we were going to hide out…

I didn't want to think about the different ways Phil Jackson might make us regret running. If Kyrie was afraid of her own brother enough to turn on him, and if he was loyal enough to the Circle of Fifths to come after his own sister, he had to be sadistic.

I didn't want to know what sadistic plans he had for once he found us.

"I know how to disappear and go off the grid," Kyrie commented. "And I know that disappearing is the only hope we have of surviving."

"This isn't the first time I've helped get an asset out," Jason added. "I specialize in difficult extractions on the New Generation Task Force," he reminded me. "Or I guess I should say I did."

"I'm sorry." The words left my mouth before I could even process that I'd said them. They were true though. Kyrie had agreed to help us despite the risk, and Jason had run with us despite having a successful career with the CIA. They had both shown that they had an unmistakable sense of what was right, and they had the strength to do the right thing, even when it was far more difficult.

Kyrie could have turned Elisabeth, Ally, and I into her brother. He would have killed us, and no one would have known. She definitely wouldn't be running for her life right now.

Kyrie shook her head. "I'm not. You took a risk. When—" her voice broke, and she swallowed to clear her throat to continue. "When Sarah's kids died, I knew I couldn't continue working for the Circle of Fifths. It didn't matter that leaving the Circle of Fifths meant leaving my family. I have seen what they are willing to do to maintain loyalty. I saw how they treated Elisabeth. I've never truly been safe. If an organization is willing to kill our children…our future, I can't be part it. I just didn't know how to get out. You gave me the opportunity."

Jason put a hand on Kyrie's back. As I tore my attention away from Kyrie and looked at Jason, I could see that it wasn't just me she was confessing to; she was confessing to her husband too. I didn't just give her the opportunity to get out of the Circle of Fifths, protect her family, and stop the Circle of Fifths from hurting any more children, but I had given her the opening she needed to come clean to her husband.

The pain on Kyrie's face, and the guarded expression that Jason was wearing screamed that they had a long way to go before the trust was repaired, but Jason's efforts to comfort Kyrie—despite the feelings he was using his training to hide—told me they would get there.

I just needed to give them time to do it.

04:37 PDT
Los Angeles, California
LAX

PHILLIP JACKSON KICKED THE TIRE of the shot-up SUV. He hadn't been happy when the Nexus had asked him to take a leave of absence from his post in the Middle East and travel to California to check on his sister. Now, he had to waste even more time tracking her down; his time was much better spent recruiting more agents, not keeping existing agents in line.

When he had heard Ally Hall's voice in his sister's house from the bugs he'd planted the day before, he knew what he needed to do. Kyrie was no longer an asset; she was a liability.

It was his job to eliminate liabilities.

The black SUV parked in front of the house when he arrived only reinforced his decision. Unfortunately, Ally hadn't been alone, and the back-up she'd brought with her was well trained. His plan for a simple one-man assassination failed spectacularly when the get away driver spotted him and warned the rest of the team.

Ally Hall needed to stop inserting herself in situations that didn't concern her. She lived in the UK now. The Circle of Fifths had effectively negated the threat Sarah Hall played in American espionage. Their only remaining threat was meant to be Dylan Hall, who, unlike his older sisters, was quite easy to manipulate. But no, Ally Hall couldn't stay away from the American Intelligence agencies.

Jackson would make sure she stayed away for good…once he found them.

05:02 PDT
Las Vegas, Nevada
Lamb Park

"WAS THIS REALLY NECESSARY?" KYRIE asked, removing the blindfold from her eyes. I had pulled my car into the garage of the house that us Halls liked to call Lamb Park, and closed the door before telling Kyrie and Jason they could take off their blindfolds.

Kalen was still asleep, so I hadn't forced a blindfold on him. That just seemed to be cruel, and borderline child abuse. If he had been awake, I wasn't sure what I would have done. He was too young to understand why he needed to put on a blindfold, but he *was* old enough (and had enough training for that matter) that if I didn't blindfold him, he could find the safehouse again.

"Already told you. It's standard policy when using a Hall safehouse." I reiterated. "I didn't make the rules. I just follow them."

"Someone needs to rethink some rules." Kyrie commented.

"A Hall safehouse is the safest place to be." Jason commented. "Maybe we should just be glad she was willing to protect us, and not question the rules." He added. "It's possible that's what makes them so safe."

Kyrie shot Jason a dirty look, but didn't say anything as she pulled Kalen out of the car.

I tried to shrug off the tension knowing I still had to get us into the house. I glanced around the garage, trying to remember all the places I'd been taught to hide a safehouse key.

Jason watched me as my eyes shot across the garage. I looked at the water heater, the shelves at the back, the sprinkler control box…

"Is everything ok?" He asked.

I nodded. "Fine. Just trying to find the key to get us inside," I replied, not letting my response distract me from my mission.

"You don't have the key?" Kyrie asked. "What was the point of bringing us to a house you don't have a key for?"

I took my attention away from looking for the potential places to hide a key, and looked at Kyrie. She looked terrified, and I could guess why.

The garage wasn't the safest place to hang out. If her brother found us, he could just shoot through the metal door, the bullets tearing through the metal like it was nothing before they eventually found our bodies. The door could be pried open. And that wasn't even considering the fact that even though it was October, the temperature in Vegas was still hot enough, staying in the non-climate controlled garage would cause dehydration at best, and heatstroke most likely. Especially for Kalen.

"There are far too many safehouses for me to have a key to every single one." I told Kyrie before going back to looking for the key. "Not to mention that we have so many safehouses in so many countries, and on so many continents that keeping the keys in a centralized location would be impossible, and beyond inconvenient."

I picked up the various paint cans from the shelf at the back of the garage, disappointed when they were all heavy enough to know they *actually* contained paint, and weren't just a plant to hide the house key.

Jason and Kyrie kept their eyes on me as I ran from one potential hiding place to another. I checked the sprinkler box and the garage door opener, my frustration starting to bubble up. It may have been a couple of years, but I was *certain* I remembered Sarah pulling the key out of a paint can, and putting it back when we left. If I could just remember...

I closed my eyes, letting the smell of the garage, and the feel of the Vegas heat take me back to the last time I was here. I focused on the parts of that trip that I could remember, letting the sing-along in the car on the way to the safehouse guide me to the moment I needed to remember. Sarah backed into the garage, closed the door, turned off the car, opened her car door, and walked to the tool box under the paint cans.

Why did she open the tool box? I could have sworn the key was in a paint can.

I opened my eyes, the fuzzy memory of what Sarah had done guiding me. I returned to the shelf, clearing the spider webs from around the tool box so I could open it. With the lid open, I inspected the tools inside. There was no way I was going to blindly shove my hand in the tool box. First of all, I didn't know what I was grabbing yet. Second, I really didn't want to risk a Brown Recluse bite because I stuck my hand in a dark tool box where it was hiding.

I had read about the effects of their venom, and there was no way I wanted to live through that torture.

The tray sitting across the top of the tool box had the most frequently used tools. There was a Philips head and flat head screw driver, as well as a rubber mallet, but no house key. Another small, shiny piece of metal caught my eye, so I picked the small tool up. It wasn't anything fancy. It looked like it was all made out of a single piece of metal, with one end looped back to create a circle like shape that then bent to a straight bar that flattened out at the other end where it looked like a flat head screw driver with a bent tip.

A paint can opener, I realized.

As I held the small tool in my hand, I could see Sarah running the loop over the lids of the paint cans. When the tool stopped in the middle of one of the lids, Sarah had taken that paint can off the shelf and opened that one.

I did as I remembered Sarah doing, and ran the loop of the paint can opener over the top of the paint cans, until the loop caught on an invisible source, pausing its movement over the lid. I used the paint can opener to slowly pry open the can. The can was full of paint, as I had already checked by picking up the cans.

Where was the key?

I took a deep breath, deciding to inspect the lid of the can. There was definitely something different about the lid, because that's what had told Sarah this can had the key. From the top it had just looked like a paint can lid, but as I looked at the inside of the lid, I found a magnetized box with paint from the can covering it.

Leave it to the Halls to hide a hide-a-key *inside* a paint can.

I grabbed the hide-a-key box so I could close the paint can and take the key with me, but it didn't move. I knew the box had a magnet, because it had caught the can opener, yet no matter the amount of force I applied to try and separate the hide-a-key from the lid, it wouldn't budge. I was frustrated, tired, and just wanted to get into the house. Glancing up at Kyrie and Jason, I could tell they felt the same. I couldn't give up now. They were counting on me.

I set the lid on the shelf with the hide-a-key facing up. With the box not moving from its place on the inside of the lid, I could guess someone reinforced the magnet with glue—most likely super glue. They wouldn't have done that unless you could open the hide-a-key without removing it. I just had to figure out how. Unfortunately, in its current paint-covered state, I couldn't see the cracks that might tell me where the door to the box sat. I could only hope I could feel them. The slimy feel of the wet paint on the plastic box caused a shiver to run down my spine while I resisted the urge to gag, but I ran my finger through it anyway until I felt the crack that indicated the door of the box, then followed the crack to get an idea of the shape of the door, hoping I could infer how to open the door once I found the shape. The top of the box had a small gap that ran about an eighth of an inch from three edges of the box. On the long edges of the box, the gap ran all the way to the short edge on the right of the box, so I dropped my finger down on that side, and found another small gap.

My guess was that the top slid open to reveal the key. I placed my thumb in the center of the lid I'd felt, placed my pointer finger on the side of the box under where the gap was, then pushed down and to the right with my thumb to slide the box open.

It didn't budge.

From the design of the box, I was positive the lid had to slide to the right. Whoever thought this box would still slide open when there was paint gluing it shut…

As much as I didn't want to gum up the blade of one of my knives, I wanted to get into the house more. Habit had me reaching for my Benchmade that I carried in my right hand back pocket, but then I thought better of it. The Ares 730S I carried in my pocket had been a present from Sarah and Neil for my 17th birthday, and was Benchmade's April Knife of the Month. The last thing I wanted to do was ruin my brand-new knife.

I glanced over my shoulder at the mini-audience I had. Kyrie had Kalen cuddled against her chest while he continued to sleep with his head on his mom's shoulder. "Jason, do me a favor and get in the glove box of the car. I need you to grab the leather knife sheath, and pull out the knife."

Jason walked over to the passenger side door, opened it, and grabbed the leather sheath from the glove box. Using one of the three blades in my Buck knife from the sheath didn't seem much better than using my Benchmade. Maybe if I didn't think too much about it, I wouldn't remember when dad brought the knife home for me, and helped me sew the sheath for it from the kit he'd picked up at the Scout store.

I turned away from Jason before the image of the sheath could immerse me in memories I couldn't get lost in at the moment. "While you're at it, can you open up the smallest blade before handing it to me?" I added, my eyes focused on the problem at hand. I stuck my left hand out as I felt Jason come up to me. I ignored the memories that pushed at my concentration as I felt the smooth wood handle in the palm of my non-paint covered hand. I couldn't think about the whittling I'd done with this knife, or the way my dad had looked at me when he walked in on me cleaning a cut I'd given myself while whittling. I slid the point of the knife through the paint where the lid needed to slide, setting the knife down on the shelf next to the can once I was done.

With the lid freed from the glue of the paint, it slid, revealing its hidden treasure beneath: the house key.

I don't think I had ever been so excited to see a plain metal house key before in my life.

I grabbed a shop towel from the shelf, and used it to wipe the paint off my right hand before grabbing the key and shoving it in my pocket. As much as I was tempted to hand the key to Jason or Kyrie so they could let us in the house, I knew there was an alarm system, and I would need to use my code to disarm it once we unlocked and opened the door.

With my hands wiped clean and the house key retrieved, I put the lid back on the paint can, and used the rubber mallet to reseal the two. Once the lid was securely on the top of the can, I put the can back on the shelf, then placed the mallet and the paint can opener back in the tool box before closing it and putting it back as well. I glanced around the garage to make sure it looked the same as it did before I began my search for the key.

I turned to let Kyrie and Jason in the house before I caught the sight of my Buck sitting on the shelf from the corner of my eye. I grabbed it, using the shop towel to wipe it clean of paint before closing it. As I slid it into my pocket, I couldn't help the quiet *Thanks dad* that sped through my thoughts.

When the door of the house swung open, the shrill warning of the alarm system greeted us, asking us to disarm it, or meet the cops. I left the door open behind me for Kyrie and Jason to follow me into the house, and walked straight up to the panel.

Blinds covered every window of the house, and they were tightly drawn, making the pale green glow from the alarm panel shine brighter than it usually would. The small digital screen reiterated what the shrill noise told me: DISARM NOW. Using the green light coming through the opaquely clear numerical buttons,

I found the correct buttons and pushed them.

4-2-5-5-2-4-0-1-#

Once I had entered all the correct keys, the beeping stopped, giving us all a reprieve from the nuisance. For the first time since getting Kyrie's phone call, I took a deep breath and relaxed.

They were safe.

For now.

As happy as I was for my momentary success, I knew I still had plenty of things to do. At the top of that list: call Ally; get some sleep.

I wouldn't be doing any of us any good if my fatigue caused a mistake that gave us away to Jackson.

I found the landline in the kitchen, picked it up, dialed the exit code 011 before the country code of 44, then put in the number I knew would connect me to Ally's private line. My call immediately went to voicemail, as I expected it would considering she was still on a plane to London. I waited until I heard the beep telling me it was recording my message, said "Camellia's at Lamb Park," and hung up.

Now it was time to get some sleep.

05:25 PDT
Los Angeles, California
Circle of Fifths SoCal Station

THE SO CAL CIRCLE OF FIFTHS station was not the thriving hive Jackson remembered... yet more evidence of his sister's betrayal. The attack on their intel gathering safehouse had devastated their California operation, and as the most senior agent at the station, it had been Kyrie's job to rebuild.

It didn't look like she had even tried.

Gaining access to Ally Hall's phone records had taken much longer than it should have, and once they did, they discovered the phone was turned off and they couldn't triangulate a location.

Fortunately, pulling her records still paid off when an alert told them someone had just tried to call her.

"That's a US number," Jackson commented, leaning over the desk of the technology expert for the team he'd commandeered to track down Kyrie and Ally. "Is that area code for a city, or a state?"

"702 is the Vegas area code," the guy replied.

"Move out," Jackson commanded. "The SUV leaves in 5 minutes." The team did as he ordered, leaving him alone with the agent at the computer. “Can you narrow down the search area, so I know where in Vegas to start searching?”

“Fortunately, the phone is registered as a landline; I can give you an address. On the downside, if they leave that location, we have no way to track them,” the agent replied.

Jackson patted his shoulder. “I’ll just have to get to them before they move, won’t I?”

10:45 PDT
Las Vegas, Nevada
Lamb Park

MY EYES SHOT OPEN. SOMETHING had changed, startling me from the light sleep I'd been getting, but I didn't know what yet. From the little light that was breaking through the tightly drawn window covers, I could tell it was still day, and I hadn't gotten more than a couple hours of sleep. I glanced at the clock on the TV tray that passed as a nightstand, only to find the screen blank.

The A/C had shut off—that was what woke me.

I was glad I'd grabbed a handgun from the floor safe in the closet before I'd fallen asleep. It made it much faster to grab it from under my pillow now that I might need it.

The hallway was empty and silent as I walked from my room to the room where I'd put Kyrie and Jason. The door was open, so I didn't waste any time knocking to announce my arrival.

"The power's out," I announced, seeing that they too were awake, while Kalen slept peacefully in the middle of the queen sized bed. "I'm going to go check it."

Kyrie's face paled. "He found us," she said.

"We don't know that," I replied. "Vegas is known for rolling brown-outs. It's a little late in the year, but you never know. There should be a back-up generator. I'm going to get us back online."

Kyrie shook her head. "No. This is Phil's M.O. He cuts the power and phone lines, then waits 90 seconds to breach. He said he enjoyed prolonging it. Either his victims have longer to panic, or it gives them enough time to hope escape is possible, before killing it."

I took a deep breath. "We better move then," I said. I stashed the gun in my waistband, then slid open the closet, looking for the release for the hidden door. When I found the support bar I was looking for, and pushed up, I heard the sliding of the mechanism that opened the door in the floor. I handed Kyrie a flashlight. "If you climb down this ladder, you'll find a tunnel at the bottom. Follow the tunnel until you find another ladder at the dead-end. Climb it, and you'll end up in a secondary safehouse a couple blocks away. There should be a car in the garage you can use to take off."

"Aren't you coming with us?" Kyrie asked.

I shook my head. "I'm going to stay here, I can buy you some time to get away again."

"Absolutely not," Kyrie replied. "It's my fault we're in this mess. I'll stay behind."

Our quiet argument became the least of our problems when the chaos of the attack broke the silence. Kyrie slammed the flashlight into my hand, grabbed her firearm, and took off, trying to buy us time by distracting the assault team. Jason picked up the still sleeping Kalen, handing him to me. "Take care of him," he told me, before turning and retrieving his weapon.

Before I could argue, I found myself standing alone in the closet that was the path to freedom, holding a sleeping seven-year-old. Jason taking off after Kyrie didn't make sense, but I could tell Jason wasn't making a logical decision. He was choosing to follow his wife to her death.

I looked at the ladder I was somehow supposed to climb down while also holding a sleeping child, and almost screamed in frustration. Unless Kalen woke up, he and I were just sitting ducks waiting for Jackson to find us.

As if Jackson heard my thoughts and wanted to prove them right, I heard the noise of a bullet traveling through a suppressor, the sound of a body crashing to the floor, and Kyrie screaming her husband's name.

I closed my eyes, hoping to block out the despair for a moment. Jason was dead…

"You betrayed the Circle of Fifths, Kyrie. You betrayed me," I heard a male voice say—Jackson. Even hidden away like I was, I could imagine Kyrie laying over her husband's body, resigned to death while her brother stalked towards her, the gun used to kill her husband now aimed at her. "How could you betray your own family?"

"You're not my family," Kyrie said. "You're a psychopath."

"Do you think it's a good idea to piss off a so called psychopath?" Jackson asked his sister.

"Does it matter? I'm already on your kill list. That's why you're here, isn't it?" Kyrie retorted.

"You betrayed the Circle of Fifths. Of course I was sent to kill you," Jackson replied, "but as long as you end up dead, they don't care how I do it, or how long I take. I plan to make you suffer."

I looked at the little boy who was finally stirring in my arms. From the little bit I knew about Jackson, I had no doubt he would use Kalen to make Kyrie suffer. Kyrie seemed resigned to death, but I knew her hope that Kalen would survive and live a good life away from the Circle of Fifths gave her the strength she was using to stand up to her brother.

The sounds of muffled voices filtered into our hiding spot, and I could tell it was Jackson talking, but I could no longer understand their conversation… I don't think I could ever forget the sound of Jackson's voice, nor the chill of danger it sent down my spine.

Especially once I heard his sister's screams of pain.

Kalen began squirming in my arms, making me look down into his confused and concerned eyes while I struggled to hold onto him. "Let me go," he commanded. "Someone is hurting mom."

"I know, bud, and I'd stop it if I could, but I can't. More than that, your mom asked me to keep you safe. I can't do that unless you climb down that ladder." Maybe it was evil to lie to Kalen about who told me to keep him safe in an effort to manipulate him into doing what I needed him to do, but I was desperate to get us out of this house. "If I set you down, will you climb down the ladder for me?"

Kalen nodded, so I began lowering him to the ground.

Suddenly, Kyrie went quiet, and Kalen began squirming as I held him against me. In my crouched position, his feet were touching the floor, giving him more leverage in his attempts to escape, but I was still stronger.

"Search the house," Jackson ordered, "Their son should be here somewhere."

The next thing I knew, Kalen threw his head back into my chin, causing my grip on him to slip, allowing him the opening he needed to wiggle free. As he ran out of the closet and towards the door of the room, I whisper yelled, "Kalen!"

Knowing there was nothing I could say to stop him, I retrieved my gun from my waist band, and followed.

I paused at the door, checking the hallway to find someone checking the room I'd been sleeping in when this attack started. I fired three rounds, just like I'd been trained, then collected his gun from the floor where it had fallen. I let off another three rounds when I reached the living room, stopping the guy that had been sneaking up on Kalen.

Kalen was bent over his mom with tears streaming down his face. "Mom, wake up."

I didn't know what Jackson had done to her, but Kyrie was covered in blood—blood that now covered Kalen as well. I made sure my gun was pointed at the floor, and removed my finger from inside the trigger guard, then approached Kalen.

I placed my left hand on his shoulder. "Kalen, she's not going to wake up. She's dead. We need to go."

The gun got pulled from my hand, causing me to spin, ready to use the self-defense moves I knew to fight my attacker. I knocked my gun from his hand, and even snuck a few more hits in. In taking the offensive, I failed to guard my head. All it took was a brief opening, but my opponent saw his opening, and snuck a punch of his own in, sending me to the ground.

My vision was swimming. I tried to get back up, but without my equilibrium I just stumbled and fell back on my hands and knees. An arm wrapped around my neck, pulling me up off the ground and restricting blood flow to my brain. I brought an arm up, trying to get it between my neck and the arm holding me, but when that didn't work, I threw my elbows back into the body attached to the arm as hard as I could.

"Stop fighting," the man hissed. I closed my eyes. It was Jackson. The same man who had just tortured and killed his own sister could kill me with just a little more pressure.

There was no way in hell I would stop fighting. Even if I stood no chance of surviving, I was going to fight for my life until I lost it. I couldn't make it easy on him.

Not to mention I had people counting on me.

Jackson's arm tightened around my neck. Apparently he didn't like being disobeyed.

Sucks to be him.

"Where's Ally?" He asked. "And why did she send a child to do her job?"

It took more effort than I had thought to find the air to form words, but I was nothing but stubborn and persistent. "This *child* has more training than most of your agents," I retorted, my voice strained from the limited air, but at least the words were recognizable. "Your agents didn't even see me coming."

"I heard six shots," Jackson commented.

"Check the bodies. All six rounds hit my targets. And if I get my hands back on my gun, I know where I'm aiming the next three rounds," I taunted.

"If all six rounds rounds hit your target, why fire so many?" Jackson replied. I could tell he was trying to put a hole in my story. He was trying to compromise my confidence.

"Check my groupings. I know you'll recognize them." I replied.

The phone started ringing, but Jackson kept me locked in place with his arm around my neck, and Kalen was frozen over his mother. The longer the phone rang, the more tension I could feel in Jackson's body as it transferred to his arm, tightening around my neck.

I needed to get out.

Instead of being smart and using Jackson's distraction to escape his grasp, I opted for the thing I did best: taunting.

"I thought Kyrie said your M.O. was to cut the phone lines?" My voice came out croaked from the extra pressure cutting off my much needed air.

"I did," Jackson snapped.

"Weird," I replied. "It's almost like this house has back-ups and decoys. I bet you're wondering right now who I could have called in the 90 seconds you waited to enter. Who is calling back? When will my back-up arrive?"

The phone stopped ringing, leaving in its wake an ominous silence.

Jackson was nervous. I could feel it in the vibration of the arm around my neck. He was talented. I would give him that. I knew he was better than me. He'd gotten the upper hand, and I didn't have enough talent to get the power balance to shift—not with pure strength and fighting talent.

But Jackson only knew what I showed him.

Right now, he was alone. His back-up was dead. That either spoke to my talent, or their inadequacy.

I hoped my taunts were augmenting my talent, but also promising I had back-up more talented than me on the way.

Based on his slight shaking, I think I was succeeding.

The phone started to ring again. I had a good idea of who it was; there was only one person who knew the safehouse was being used. The ringing of the phone told me what time it was, and the person calling with one annoying tone.

We left LAX almost eleven hours ago. Ally was off the plane, had checked her messages, and was calling to check-in. She wasn't going to stop calling until someone picked up.

She was going to be so mad when she found out that I put her on the plane with a promise I'd be safe, then got myself killed.

If I could defeat Jackson, maybe she wouldn't have to know how close I really was to dying.

"Who's on the phone?" Jackson asked, his voice a whisper right next to my ear.

I thought I had done a good job hiding my anxiety to answer the phone. Apparently not.

"I know Ally Hall was involved in sending my sister on the run, which stands to reason, this is a Hall safehouse. But not just anyone can use a Hall safehouse," Jackson posited.

I closed my eyes. The phone stopped ringing. My plan had backfired.

"You can't be more than what? 18? I don't believe you are as capable as you are trying to make me believe, but I can't ignore the fact that you took down two well trained CIA operatives. Outside of the Circle of Fifths, I only know one family that trains children."

The phone started ringing again, and Jackson started to make his way towards it, dragging me with him.

"Tell me, how are you related to Ally? Cousin? Niece?"

Jackson picked up the phone, but didn't say anything. I recognized what he was trying to do. Usually it wouldn't work. Not on Ally or any of my other siblings. But I knew Ally was already on edge after what happened to Sarah's kids. She was concerned about me, and I sent her away from where she could help me. Now I had left her call unanswered. Twice. Even though the phone wasn't up to my ear, I could still hear Ally's voice through the phone.

"Emily Nour Hall. You know better. You answer the phone. You don't send me to voicemail. Ever. Especially not when you are protecting assets from the Circle of Fifths."

It didn't matter that I couldn't see Jackson's face. Before he replied to Ally, I knew he was happy.

"So her name's Emily. I'll admit, I'd already figured out she was a Hall. Unfortunately, your assets are already dead," Jackson replied.

There was a pause on the other side of the line. Yeah, if Jackson didn't kill me, Ally would once I got home. "If you killed my sister, there will be—"

If I could shake my head, I would have. So much for Ally's years of training. All it had taken was a couple years being locked up behind the security afforded a title holder in England, and my sister was giving away intel like she was a teacher giving her students a study guide for a test.

"Oh, Emily's not dead—yet. It would be quite fitting, don't you think. For me to take your sister from you, like you took my sister from me…" Jackson trailed off, letting the severity of his threat wash over both me and Ally.

I wanted to point out that it wasn't Ally's fault his sister was dead. Technically, I was the one who recruited her as an asset, but I hadn't killed her—he had. But with his arm wrapped around my neck, squeezing tight, talking was exceptionally difficult, and I didn't think it wise to waste my energy pointing out something that would likely get me killed.

"Fortunately for your sister, she just became a valuable resource to me. You see, as much as I love the karma of killing your sister as revenge for causing my sister's death, I know it would just give you more motivation to come after me. I would prefer to get rid of problems, not create more, so I will propose to you a trade: give me your life, to save hers."

No no no no no. This could not be happening. I knew Ally. It didn't matter that the deal sucked. It didn't matter that she would be giving Jackson exactly what he wanted. It didn't matter that by turning herself over to Jackson, she was helping the Circle of Fifths. I was Ally's little sister, and at the end of the day, I knew that she would do everything she could to save me.

Even as I heard the line disconnect, I knew that Ally would do exactly what Jackson had told her to do. And when the arm around my neck tightened, and my vision started going black, I knew there was nothing I could do to stop it.

I had failed, but Ally would pay the price.

TOP SECRET PROMISING GENERATION EYES ONLY

Operation Subversion
Objective: Systematically dismantle the Circle of Fifths

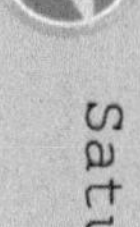

FIELD REPORT: 21 October 2000

CLASSIFIED TOP SECRET

02:43 BST Feilds Palace; Twickenham, London
00:21 PDT CoF So Cal Station; Los Angeles, CA
13:43 BST Feilds Palace; Twickenham, London
15:27 PDT CoF So Cal Station; Los Angeles, CA
18:17 PDT CoF So Cal Station; Los Angeles, CA

02:43 BST
Twickenham, London
Feilds Palace

NO MATTER HOW HARD ALLY tried, she couldn't slink into sleep. Michael had fallen asleep on his back, and despite the bed they shared being king-sized, Ally laid with her head on his chest. His arm cuddled her to him, and if it were any other night, she would feel safe and protected. She rarely let her walls down to be vulnerable with someone, but Michael was her home. The small family they were building was quickly becoming her safe haven.

Tonight it felt like a suffocating prison instead.

Ally slipped Michael's arm off of her before sliding out of the blankets. She padded through their suite until she reached Kate's crib. She took a deep breath, watching her little girl sleep. The way Kate was curled up in the crib told Ally that it was time to start transitioning Kate into a toddler bed. It didn't seem like it had been four years since she'd last found out she was pregnant. It felt like yesterday she had gone to an appointment without Michael, because he was busy, and found out she was carrying twins. Sometimes, she was still haunted by the decision she had made to hide

Lynn from everyone, including Michael, at MI6. Especially when she'd had a rough few days like she'd just had. She wanted nothing more than to hug both of her girls and remember why she was fighting for a better world.

Subconsciously, her hand found her way to her still flat stomach. Seeing Sarah's family blown apart had her wishing she could have her entire family together, at least once. She couldn't imagine the child she was carrying not growing up with Kate, or maybe even Lynn. Even in three short years, she could tell that her girls were going to grow up to be fierce protectors.

Ally tensed as she felt a set of arms wrap around her waist, relaxing when she glanced behind her to see Michael.

"I didn't mean to wake you," Ally apologized.

Michael shook his head as he set his chin on her shoulder, watching Kate sleep with his wife. "You aren't the only one who couldn't sleep. I care for Emily too, you know."

Ally took a deep breath. "I can't let her die."

"No one wants Emily to die," Michael replied, "but I want you to live too."

"If you had to choose between her and me, who would you choose?" Ally whispered. "Because I would choose her," she admitted.

"If I asked you to choose between me and Rafael, who would you choose?" Michael retorted. He took a deep breath. "It won't come to that. You have the weight of two intelligence agencies behind you. We'll find her and save her without having to sacrifice yourself to do so."

Ally nodded and let herself melt into her husband's arms, savoring the moment even though she knew her husband was wrong. She had grown up watching as her dad tried to track down the Circle of Fifths for the CIA. Even with the joint wrath of the CIA and MI-6, they hadn't been able to prevent the Circle of Fifths from killing Michael's mum.

Ally couldn't let history repeat itself.

Michael was right though. She couldn't sacrifice herself to the Circle of Fifths. She had children to raise, including one that would die if she died. Even though she was willing to sacrifice her life so her sister could live, she couldn't sacrifice the life of her baby for her sister's life.

00:21 PDT
Los Angeles, California
Circle of Fifths SoCal Station

HAVING GROWN UP IN A family fighting against the Circle of Fifths, I knew that the Circle of Fifths didn't take prisoners. Until I found myself restrained in their SoCal station, I didn't appreciate what that truly meant. When I woke up from my oxygen-deprivation-caused sleep, I was tied up with cobbled together materials—I didn't know which was more uncomfortable: the rope I'd been tied up with for Promising Generation training, or the computer cords currently cutting off the blood supply to my hands.

While their choice of hand-tying materials talked to their inexperience taking hostages, watching the effortless way they covered up Kyrie and Jason's murders proved their experience getting away with murder.

Jackson got back from his sister's house—where he had staged a home invasion and double homicide then played the devastated brother when he called the cops—and threw Kalen at me. "Fix him," he ordered.

"Excuse me?" I replied.

Jackson spun back at me. "You heard me. Fix him. His water works were useful for the interview with the cops, but now that we're back, I need him to get it together so I can start training him."

"He's a child," I said. "He just lost both of his parents. He's going to need therapy, and a loving, guiding hand to help him get through this. Not *training*."

"Is that what your sister did with her kid?" Jackson asked, a taunting tone entering his voice. "What's her name again? You know, the one who killed her siblings."

"She didn't kill her siblings. The Circle of Fifths did." I replied.

Jackson got really close to my face. "It doesn't matter, does it? I've seen the confession. She believes she killed her siblings. Just like Kalen believes he killed his parents. It makes them moldable. Don't try to tell me your sister hasn't used their deaths as motivation to convince *Alyxandrie* to take your Promising Generation training more seriously. Your sister just lost three kids. Don't try to tell me they are coddling their last surviving child—the reason they lost *all* their other kids—and giving her *all* of the love and guidance she needs."

I couldn't say anything. I couldn't be sure that Sarah and Neil didn't blame Vee for Cole and Analyn's deaths. What I did know, was they definitely weren't giving her any love or guidance.

But I was. And so were Madelyn and Deputy Director McLean.

Who was going to support Kalen? Not his uncle. Was Jackson his guardian now?

"How am I supposed to help Kalen calm down if I have my hands tied behind my back?" I asked. Maybe, just maybe, if I could convince them to untie me, and leave me alone with Kalen, I could find a way to escape and take him with me. Kyrie died to protect Kalen from the Circle of Fifths. I had to do what ever I could to make sure her sacrifice wasn't for nothing.

13:43 BST
Twickenham, London
Feilds Palace

ALLY USED THE TIPS OF her fingers to massage her forehead toward her temples. She felt the start of a tension headache pulsing, but had yet to find something that would have made it worth it. She needed something, *anything* she could use to find Emily.

"I need ibuprofen," Ally sighed under her breath.

Tyson Barnes looked up from the reports he was combing through. "I'm sorry, I didn't quite catch that."

"I need ibuprofen," she repeated. She turned to Michael who was flipping through intelligence reports on her right. "Do we have any?"

Michael looked up, an answer on his lips as Barnes interrupted instead: "Is Ibuprofen really good for your—"

"Finish that sentence, Tyson. I dare you. If you ask me O*ne. More. Time.* what would be good for my baby, I will kill you. Nothing about our current situation is good for an easy pregnancy, but neither is this stress-induced headache, so get me some ibuprofen, or Tylenol—acetaminophen, paracetamol—whatever it's called. Just get me something for this headache before I can't think and my sister dies because of it."

Michael grabbed Ally's hand. "Let's go get some lunch."

"No. Not until we figure out where the psychopath is keeping my sister," Ally replied, pulling her hand from Michael's while turning back to her stack of reports.

"I thought we already agreed that we weren't sacrificing your life for Emily's," Michael prodded.

Ally didn't respond, maintaining a laser focus on the papers in front of her.

"Come on, darling. You're not going to help Emily by starving yourself. Let's go get you food and something for your headache. Tyson can continue to go through the files, and let us know what he finds when we get back."

Michael's offer was tempting. She had skipped breakfast in favor of searching these files. If she was being honest with herself, her headache was probably a result of not eating, or drinking, and spending *far* too long staring at the tiny black lines on the white paper. But she couldn't give up. Her brain was all too happy to supply images of the many ways Kyrie's brother could be torturing Emily… finding Emily would be saving Ally just as much as it saved Emily.

Her phone rang, and she grabbed it, grateful for the distraction it gave her both from the loop in her own brain, as well as Michael's tempting offer. "This is Feilds."

"Where is Emily?" Sarah asked from the other side.

Ally's eyes slid closed. She'd known this was a risk when she decided not to tell Sarah she was taking Emily with her to California. When Emily was taken, she'd known that her siblings would be furious if they found out. "Sarah, I can explain," Ally started.

"Oh, you will. How about you start with the fact that you called the school pretending to be me, and excused her from school? When I got the call yesterday, asking if she was still sick, I said yes, assuming it was Madilyn who had called in the absence. When I got back to the house and discovered she left with you Wednesday night…"

Ally let out a measured breath. Sarah didn't know that the Circle of Fifths had Emily. For the time being, that was probably a good thing. With her current mental state, Sarah would cause more harm than good. After all, she didn't have her CIA clearance anymore, and she would go charging down to Las Vegas with no plan.

It was rare that Ally straight up lied to her twin. There were plenty of secrets the two of them had kept from everyone else, but the two of them…

When Cole had shown up in London, all Ally had to do was not contact her sister, and that had been more difficult than she could have imagined. If she was going to make sure she had a real chance to get Emily back, she was going to just straight up lie to Sarah. Having never lied to her twin before, Ally wasn't sure if Sarah would actually believe her.

"I needed her help with something. It was only supposed to take a day, but it took longer than I thought. I will have her back in time for school on Monday," Ally promised.

Fortunately, Sarah seemed to buy the lie. "You can't just take Emily out of school any time its…"

Sarah continued talking, but Ally didn't hear what she was saying after Tyson announced "I've got something."

"Sorry Sarah, but I've got to go," Ally said before hanging up on her sister. Sarah would be pissed at her, but she could wait to yell at her until after she found Emily and got her home.

Ally got up from her seat at the table, and walked around to where Tyson was going though his stack of papers. "What did you find?"

"We needed something to tell us where Jackson went after Vegas, and I think I found it. The police in Chino Hills are currently looking for suspects in a fatal home invasion," Tyson replied.

"How is that useful? They left Chino Hills when Michael and I did, and headed to Vegas. We *know* they made it to Vegas."

"The victims of the fatal home invasion were Jason and Kyrie McKenzie. The report says Kyrie's brother Phillip Jackson found their seven-year-old son crying over their bodies when he went over for their weekly dinner."

"So he took them back to SoCal," Ally breathed.

Tyson turned to look at Ally. "We have long suspected they have a base in that region of California. It's likely he took her there."

Ally nodded her head. She was almost certain that was where Jackson took her. After all, he didn't live in California, and he made his sister's house a crime scene. A Circle of Fifths base would be the best and most secure place to hide a prisoner. She turned to Michael. "I think I'd like to take you up on that offer of lunch," she said.

Michael took her hand and led her out of the room, leaving Tyson to try and figure out where the Circle of Fifths base might be. Once the door closed on the room, leaving Ally and Michael out of Tyson's hearing, Ally stopped walking.

"Can I meet you in the kitchen?" Ally asked. "I want to check in on Kate."

Michael kissed Ally's forehead. "I'll see you in a minute," he replied.

Ally nodded, watching as he walked towards the kitchen. When he turned the corner, Ally squared her shoulders. Tyson wouldn't be able to find the Circle of Fifths base… not fast enough. Fortunately Ally had ideas on how she could get that answer *much* faster.

15:27 PDT
Los Angeles, California
Circle of Fifths So Cal Station

DESPITE MY EFFORTS, I HAD yet to get Jackson to untie me, or leave me alone with Kalen. Unfortunately, I had proved myself wrong, and somehow got Kalen to stop crying, therefore ruining any leverage I had to convince Jackson to untie me.

I watched from my wall-less prison cell as Jackson sparred with Kalen across the room. All of the agents I had seen since arriving had slowly been sent out on other assignments, until it was just Jackson watching me. I was getting the sense that he didn't trust me. Then again, I was tied up, so that was a given. Insisting he was the one to stay and watch me implied he didn't trust the Circle of Fifths agents either. At the very least, he didn't trust that they could keep me from escaping.

If ever there was a time to be underestimated, it was now. My plan from Vegas had backfired so spectacularly and I was suffering the consequences.

My eyes shot over to the phone sitting on the back desk of what I could only assume was once a thriving Circle of Fifths command center. Every time the phone had rung up to this point, one of the agents got sent out on assignment. If the pattern held, the Circle of Fifths had another task for their So Cal station agents to complete.

And there was only one agent left.

I took some deep breaths as Jackson approached the phone. My opportunity to escape was quickly approaching, but I couldn't let my excitement sabotage that chance.

"Jackson." He answered the phone with the same clipped tone he had used the first several times he'd answered the phone.

I couldn't hear what was being said from where I was tied up, but the way Jackson's eyes migrated to me, I knew that they had another assignment for the SoCal team. I also knew that I was right to hide my excitement, because even with a bored, passive look on my face, I could see that the last thing Jackson wanted to do was leave me alone.

"All of our SoCal agents are currently out on other assignments," Jackson reported. His gaze left me as he continued, "but as soon as one of them return, I will send someone."

My stomach fell hearing Jackson's report. I was tied up for crying out loud. How much trouble did he think I was capable of?

I mean, I wanted him to leave because I knew I would have a much better chance of escape, so his concerns were most likely warranted, but still.

What was the world coming to if a girl couldn't get away with things because her enemies underestimated her?

"The SoCal office is not as strong as Kyrie's reports led us to believe. It's running with a skeleton crew which apparently hasn't been rebuilt since the Icarus Incident."

My heart started pounding. *How on earth did Jackson know the Promising Generation File name for Cole and Annie's deaths?* When he had mentioned Vee's police interview, I hadn't thought much of it. After all, the copy the Promising Generation had in Icarus was just one of many. But to know the incident code name?

When I got out of here, I needed to make sure *everyone* who was a Circle of Fifths mole got moved away from the Promising Generation.

I would hate manipulating Peter's dad out of his life, knowing his mom was already being removed, but I had a feeling it would be better for him in the long run.

"Yes sir, I understand what high priority means. It will be the first assignment given as soon as one of the agents get back." Jackson told the person on the other side of his phone call.

My hopes were slowly sinking by the second. *Curse Vegas-Emily and her plan to escape.*

"No sir, I do not think I am above completing assignments. I briefed you on the situation when I arrived—"

Now that was interesting. How much of this *situation* had Jackson briefed the Circle of Fifths on? I already didn't trust that Jackson would let me go once he got Ally.

The Circle of Fifths didn't take prisoners.

Letting me go would cause vulnerabilities in the Circle of Fifths. After all, I now knew where their So Cal station was. If I had to guess what would happen, Jackson would incapacitate Ally, kill me in front of her, torture her to get what information he could from her, then kill her.

If the Circle of Fifths knew I was here, I had no doubt that my death was inevitable.

As whoever was on the other side of the call talked, Jackson looked at me again. Based on the look on his face, he hadn't told the Circle of Fifths I was here, and he was wishing he had.

"Understood, sir. I'm leaving now." Jackson's words echoed through my head long after I heard the click of the phone being returned to its cradle.

A huge weight lifted off my chest. For the first time since Vegas, I felt hope that I might actually live and save my sister.

For the first time since Vegas, I finally had a plan solidifying in my mind that might actually work.

"Kalen, you're coming with me," Jackson announced, grabbing a set of keys from wall.

No, no, no, no.

I tried to hide my panic, but as I glanced at Jackson, I could tell I wasn't doing a very good job of it. His smirk was louder than any threat he could make. He knew my plan. He knew I was capable of escaping.

He knew if I escaped with Kalen, he wouldn't find us again. He knew if I escaped, he would lose his chance to capture Ally. He was making me choose: stay and try to find another opportunity to escape with Kalen but risk my sister's life, or escape now to save my sister and doom Kalen to a life with his uncle.

Jackson ushered Kalen out the door, throwing another smirk over his shoulder to me as he closed the door behind him. As the door clicked shut, I thrashed in my chair, screaming out my frustration.

I hung my head, warm tears falling off my cheeks into my lap.

I hated Jackson. I hated Jackson for making me choose—not because it was a hard choice. I already knew what I was going to do; I hated myself for the choice I was going to make.

I hated Jackson for showing me the worst part of myself.

18:17 PDT
Los Angeles, California
Circle of Fifths So Cal Station

THE TEMPTATION TO SCREAM AT the empty station in frustration was pounding in my throat like the bass at some of the underground parties I had snuck into before moving to Virginia. I had expended far more effort than I had predicted I'd need to escape, and I was still tied to this stupid chair.

If you think the curse words, you'll say the curse words, and if you say the curse words, Vee will hear you, and if Vee hears you, she'll copy you, and if her mom hears those words come out of her baby's mouth, she will never leave you alone with her again.

My inner monologue that usually kept me from resorting to explicatives to express my frustration wasn't working nearly as well as it usually did.

Especially not when the thoughts that followed it were, *if you don't die here.*

It hadn't taken me long to realize that the computer cords were very different from the rope I'd been trained with. Rope was flexible. It had some give, which I had used time and time again to gain the leverage I needed to work on the knots, and slip from its bonds. I had trained for it over, and over, *and over,* until I could escape from being tied up without much thought.

The computer cords had none of the same flexibility. Knowing their construction, it made sense. Instead of thousands of nylon fibers being twisted together to create a strong length of material to hold weight, computer cords had metal wires twisted together inside a plastic tube of insulation. They were designed to transmit information and power along its lengths, not be twisted in on itself to hold captives. I did not envy the power cord tamer who had formed the knots that now held me.

Then again, I took solace in the fact that tying me up had taken quite a bit of effort.

I had spent the better part of the last two hours trying to escape from the knots, and I felt as though all of my efforts had been in vain. I had tried working the computer cords like I would rope to untie the knots. Then I'd tried to force the knots to loosen and give me enough room to slip through them.

When my training had failed, I looked around the space, and located a pair of scissors…all the way across the room, with several desk, chairs, and other obstacles in my way.

I knew from looking at the chair I was in and the others, that all of the office chairs in this station sat on a single gas lift leg, with five casters branching off at the bottom. My feet were tied together around one of the casters, leaving me with very minimal room to spin in the chair, but left with just enough movement with my feet to walk the chair where I wanted to go.

If I thought the inexperience of these agents at taking hostages meant it would be easier for me to escape, I was wrong. They may not have had a metal chair and rope to tie me up, but what they had used was effective. Sure, they had tied me to a rolling office chair, but either they had removed one of the wheels before tying me up, or they made sure they tied me up in the one broken chair. Either way, my progress towards the scissors I'd found was slow and tedious.

As I finally felt the smooth plastic handle of the pair of scissors under my hand, my anxiety about how long I was taking to escape got louder. The longer it took me to escape, the higher the probability was that someone would return, and at two hours, I didn't like my odds.

It was a tedious process trying to cut through the plastic and metal that bound my hands together, but finally, I felt the scissors jolt through the cord, freeing one of my hands. I took the scissors in my now free hand, and brought it to my lap, testing the other hand to see if it would move, or if it was tied to the chair. Fortunately it wasn't, and I brought my left hand, with cords still tied around it, to my lap.

I decided to worry about getting the cords off my hand later, and redirected my attention to my feet. I could get the cords off my hand as I ran, but I couldn't run toward freedom until I freed my legs from the broken chair.

With my arms free to move around, I was able to bend over and look at my feet, making it much easier to use the scissors to cut through the cords tying my feet to the chair. Before I knew it, I was standing and stretching my muscles as I made my way towards the door I had seen all the other agents use to leave on their missions. I hadn't seen anyone use any sort of code or key to leave, so I was hoping it would be easy for me to just walk out the front door.

I held the scissors pointed out in front of me, in case I met someone on the other side of the door, and pushed it open. Nothing prevented it from opening; no alarm sounded. I found myself in an underground parking garage, where the last vestiges of the evening light shone down the ramp.

I tucked the scissors in my back pocket—just in case, and ran. I sprinted towards the dark red light of the sunset, knowing that my escape would prevent my sister's death. With every step I took, I felt the failure of leaving Kalen behind, but the hope of my sister living grew.

As long as I was alive, and free, I would do everything I could to save Kalen.

But in order to save him, I had to save myself first.

The ramp leading outside was in reach, when I heard the sound of a car starting down the ramp. I ducked to the side, using a pillar to hide. But when the car reached the parking arm at the bottom, I heard the driver pull the parking brake, and the car door opened. The sound of footsteps on the concrete floor echoed off the walls of the surrounding garage, making it difficult for me to identify exactly where the newcomer was.

Difficult, but not impossible.

I shifted my position around the pole as the agent got closer, making sure I was out of his eye site at all times. Once he'd passed me, I pulled the scissors out of my back pocket, and with light feet to avoid making noise, I charged at the agent. I needed as much time as possible to put distance between me and the Circle of Fifths, so the last thing I needed was this agent calling Jackson before I was even out of the parking garage.

Before the scissors could even make an impact, the agent caught my wrist and pulled the scissors from my hand.

My time tied up made me even weaker than I'd thought.

With the scissors, or not, I was not going to be defeated… not this time.

I pulled my wrist free of the agents grasp, using the momentum of pulling it free to launch my other fist towards his stomach. I didn't need my dominant hand to land a breathtaking punch, and this agent was about to find that out the hard way.

Sure enough, my fist connected and the agent lost his breath with a curse. Before I could even acknowledge the very *British* swear coming from my opponent, the scissors clattered to the ground, and I found both of my wrists being held.

"Emily. Stop. Ally sent me," a deep baritone voice I recognized ordered.

I looked up at the face of the man I'd been attacking, paying attention to more than my need to escape for the first time. As I stared into eyes the same color green as my brother-in-law, the older version of a man I'd met when I was five began to remove the cords still dangling from my left wrist. "Rafael?" I asked.

I hated how small and broken my voice came out. I hated that the smallest bit of hope that I was finally safe, caused the adrenaline—and the strength it'd been fueling—to drain away.

Worst of all, I hated the fact that I didn't know if I could trust Rafael… but I was too weak, and *solely* at his mercy.

Rafael finished freeing my wrist, grabbing the cords and the scissors with one hand, before putting the other on my back to lead me back to his car. "We'll call your sister from the car. She won't sleep until she knows you're safe."

I let Rafael lead me to his car, which was still running on the public side of the parking gate. All of the fight I'd had minutes before was gone, letting him open the door and help me into the passenger seat without so much as an argumentative word from me. I felt my eyes start to slide close with the door, and when I reopened them, Rafael was in the drivers seat, handing me a phone.

"You know Ally's number?" He asked.

I nodded in response, too lazy to try to form a verbal response.

"Good. Call her and let her know you're alive. Then you can sleep," Rafael told me.

I grabbed the phone and dialed Ally's number, trying not to

think about what happened the last time I'd called her, then taken a nap.

The phone call connected, and I heard Ally's voice answer: "This is Feilds."

"It's Emily," I said.

"Oh thank goodness. How are you? Never mind, that's a stupid question. Did Jackson hurt you?" Ally's questions streamed from the phone faster than I could process them, never mind answer them.

"I'm fine. I escaped, and Rafael is driving me…" I trailed off, realizing I never asked where Rafael was taking me.

"To Virginia." Two voices answered me: one from next to me in the car, and the other through the phone. So Ally had sent Rafael for me, and they'd discussed a plan for once he found me. I took comfort in the fact that Ally trusted Rafael, because I had no choice but to trust him at the moment.

"Jackson has Kalen," I admitted softly, unsure if the phone would carry my words to my sister. "I failed. I failed Kylie. I failed Kalen. I failed Cole. I failed Vee."

"You haven't failed until you give up," Ally told me. "I don't know about you, but I'm not giving up. Occasionally we need to take a step back to regroup, but I will *never* give up."

I took a deep breath. I knew Ally was right, but it was hard to see that from where I sat now. I'd used up all of my hope escaping. It had taken everything in me just to save myself. How was I supposed to go back up against Jackson? How was I supposed to go back up against the Circle of Fifths? It had taken everything I had to escape. How was I supposed to save Kalen too?

"Get some rest, Em." The way Ally told me to take care of myself… she sounded so much like our mother. "You did the hard part. Let me take a turn."

TOP SECRET PROMISING GENERATION EYES ONLY

Operation Subversion
Objective: Systematically dismantle the Circle of Fifths

FIELD REPORT:22 October 2000

CLASSIFIED TOP SECRET

07:25 MDT I-40; Albuquerque, NM
07:35 MDT Adventure Alley Store 428; Albuquerque, NM
07:40 MDT Adventure Alley Store 428; Albuquerque, NM
07:55 MDT Adventure Alley Store 428; Albuquerque, NM
08:15 MDT ABQ Int. Sunport Rental; Albuquerque, NM

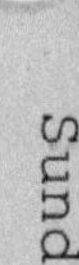

07:25 MDT
Albuquerque, New Mexico
I-40

SLEEPING WHILE TRAVELING FELT ODDLY like teleportation. I couldn't remember exactly where I fell asleep, but I knew we were sitting in LA traffic. When a rumble strip roused me from sleep, the sun was rising on the horizon, casting the first rays of light over a tan expanse of desert.

"I didn't mean to wake you," Rafael said, glancing at me in the passenger seat. "But since you're awake…"

Rafael handed me granola bar, which I thankfully took. I peeled open the wrapper, taking a bite as I watched the barren landscape pass the window, trying to figure out where we were. Unfortunately, the deserts of California, Nevada, Arizona, New Mexico, and Texas looked very similar. Not even the signs were useful. They told me that we were heading East on I-40, and we were 125 miles from a city called Santa Rosa, but when most of the South West was settled by Spanish speakers, it didn't help me narrow it down at all.

I put the last bite of the granola bar in my mouth. With the way I'd scarfed it down, I must have been starving, but I'm not sure why that surprised me. Jackson hadn't exactly fed me very well while I was his hostage, so I was pretty sure my last decent meal had been the dinner with Ally and Michael I'd left to meet with Kyrie and Elisabeth.

I didn't even know how long ago that was. Time had somehow compressed since then, so it somehow felt like mere hours separated me from those memories; at the same time it felt like months.

Then again, when I went to sleep, it had been sunset. Now it was sunrise. At this time of year, the nights weren't short. And it wasn't the first time in the last few days I'd lost time by sleeping. For all I knew, I'd lost far more time than I could even begin to estimate.

"Where are we?" I finally asked. Maybe I had just been beaten down too much recently, but I didn't exactly trust my deduction skills at the moment. To begin with, I couldn't even trust myself enough to figure out how long I'd been asleep, so how could I possibly try to figure out how far we'd gone while I was asleep?

"New Mexico," Rafael answered. "We'll be driving through Albuquerque soon."

I nodded, looking back out the window.

"Before we get to Albuquerque, we need to stop. Ally told me there should be an Adventure Alley before we hit the city proper. Now that you're awake, I'm hoping you can help with the script."

My head shot back to Rafael, my eyes narrowing. If someone dug deep enough, they would discover that my family owned the over 600 Adventure Alley Travel Stores that were placed along most of the main interstates in the country. Our ownership of the gas station and convenience store chain was a well hidden—and closely guarded—secret, and for good reason too. My parents had made an investment in their first store as a way to earn the funds to purchase their first safehouse. But as Adventure Alley expanded, it became more than just a way to fund our safehouse network; it became a modern day Underground Railroad for spies.

The travel stores were placed along the interstates because that made motorists more likely to use them. Their location also made them the perfect place to stash anything a spy family like ours might need if they needed to disappear. Every location had a small building off the back; there was a garage with a car, a closet with spare clothes, a safe with cash, a bathroom with a shower, and a couple of rooms with beds. The key to the mini safehouse was under the till in one of the registers, and could be retrieved if someone knew what to say and do.

"Exactly what did Ally tell you?" I asked Rafael.

Rafael took a deep breath. "The Adventure Alleys are how we are going to check in with Ally. We are supposed to change clothes and cars in Albuquerque, then we'll drive on through to the Fort Smith location in Arkansas, where we will sleep for a few hours before switching cars and changing clothes again. Our last car change will be in Kodak, Tennessee right before we switch from I-40 to I-81 and enter Virginia."

I wasn't sure what to say. Rafael had a detailed plan for getting me back to the McLean's house, and he had knowledge about a network of stores that not even Neil's parents knew about... clearly Ally trusted him, but as far as I knew, he was working with the Circle of Fifths. "Why does Ally trust you?" I asked quietly.

Rafael glanced at me briefly, but maintained a focus on driving. "Ally is my handler," he answered.

"Since when?" I asked. I knew that Ally had her secrets, and I had been painfully reminded of that fact when she told me Cole was alive. But Rafael...

"Since the Circle of Fifths killed my mum," Rafael answered.

I stared at Rafael incredulously. The Circle of Fifths had killed Rafael and Michael's mother in 1988, when they'd been trying to convince Thomas, their father, to join them. I had always known that was Rafael's tipping point. He'd fallen in love with Nika, who was a member of Russian Intelligence. The conversation where Rafael revealed to his father his intention to propose hadn't gone well, so when his mum died, he blamed his dad.

It had always made sense when he gave up his claim to the family title, left the UK, and married Nika. I had always believed the rumors that he joined the Circle of Fifths as well. After all, there had been a few occasions where the Russians had gotten their hands on classified US Intelligence, and the Circle of Fifths benefited from the Russian's actions. Rafael was the puzzle piece I had always assumed explained it.

"I always assumed you joined the Circle of Fifths because you were pissed at your father," I admitted.

Rafael nodded his head. "That's what I needed people to believe." He took a deep breath. "When I found out that my mother had paid the price for my father's resistance to the Circle of Fifths, I was livid. I yelled, said some not so nice things, then stormed off."

"I was there, remember?" I interrupted. "I may not have a ton of memories from when I was five, but that one… I remember everything about that day. I remember you and Michael arguing, and then you storming off. I was also there when Ally calmed Michael down and convinced him to let her talk to you. I watched as she left, and I was there when she came back and told us she couldn't find you."

"She found me," Rafael admitted quietly. "And *knocked some sense into me*, as she called it. Ally knows how to fight, but only fought me long enough to convince me to listen. The conversation that followed refocused my anger onto the peoples responsible for my mother's death, and I began questioning Ally about what was being done to stop the Circle of Fifths…"

I remained quiet as Rafael trailed off. If that day was important and impactful enough to be ingrained into my 5-year-old memory, I was certain Rafael had that conversation memorized. I could just about imagine the conversation replaying in his head as he relayed it to me.

Oh what I would give to have witnessed that conversation.

"You weren't satisfied with her answer," I guessed when the silence dragged on for a moment too long.

Rafael nodded. "We argued. I've only ever seen Ally lose her cool one time, and it was when she said if I wasn't happy with what was being done about the Circle of Fifths, I should do something."

"She wasn't serious, but you were," I finished for him.

"My relationship with my father was already strained, and tabloid reporters had picked up on it. I knew when I proposed to Nika, the resulting fallout with my family would be broadcast on the covers of the tabloids, perhaps even here in the states. I knew if I just let it all happen, I would be perfectly positioned to give the Circle of Fifths something that they wanted, something that not even my father could give them." We passed a sign directing us to take the next exit for the Adventure Alley.

The car returned to silence, and I bit my tongue not to interrupt it as Rafael drove the last mile before the exit. As the car slowed down the ramp for the stop sign at the bottom, I quietly asked the question I desperately wanted answered: "Who knows?"

"Ally, Nika, my father…" Rafael glanced at me as the car stopped at the stop sign. "And you."

I expected the list to be short… but not that short. I mean, Michael wasn't even on the list, and he was Rafael's *brother*.

Rafael pulled into the Adventure Alley, and parked in front of one of the gas pumps. "Are you going to be ok getting the key by yourself?" He asked me.

"Yeah. Being by myself might be easier, but what are you going to do while I'm getting the key?" I asked.

"I'm going to fill the gas tank." Rafael replied.

"Why?" I asked. "I thought you said we were switching cars here."

"We are, but I need to get rid of the rental. The plan was for you to drive the car we pick up, and follow me to drop off the rental in Albuquerque," Rafael told me. "Are you awake enough to follow me?"

"Yeah, I'll be fine," I promised.

Rafael looked me over carefully, as if judging for himself whether I was ready to be left alone for even a moment. I could see the concern in his eyes...a concern that wasn't dissimilar to what I'd seen in my father's eyes before he died, or the concern my brother and brother-in-laws had shown me since.

It was weird.

Once Rafael had decided I was telling the truth, he nodded. "Come get me once you've retrieved the key."

Before Rafael changed his mind, I walked toward the convenience store portion of the Adventure Alley.

Time to see if I remembered my training.

07:35 MDT
Albuquerque, New Mexico
Adventure Alley Store 428

A BELL CHIMED AS I pulled the door open towards me, but as I stepped through Adventure Alley's doors, I was greeted by quiet. As I walked to the check-out desk where the cashier sat, eyes scanning the text of a Clive Cussler novel, I couldn't help but notice I was the only customer in the store.

I wanted to kick myself for not paying attention to the fact that there weren't any cars in the parking lot. I was on the run from a dangerous organization of terrorists. Knowing how many cars were in the parking lot, what the makes and models of the cars were, and what their drivers and passengers looked like was much more important for my escape and survival than identifying the song playing softly over the store's intercom as *NSYNC's "Bye Bye Bye," or the novel the cashier was reading as the most recent Dirk Pitt novel *Atlantis Found.*

Technically, I had been trained to observe all of those things. Being hyper-aware of all of my surroundings would help me notice patterns that might reveal a tail, and small details like what song was playing, and what book the cashier was reading would help me forge a relationship with the cashier. The more connected to and comfortable with me I could make the cashier feel, the more likely she was to help me, or reveal something that might be helpful, but otherwise wouldn't.

I veered off towards the Grab'n'go breakfast items. Even though there was likely food I could grab in the bunker out back, I couldn't hide the fact that I was starving, and it gave me an excuse to linger in the store for a bit before approaching the check stand. Under the guise of considering my convenience store breakfast options, I watched the cashier, using the small clues surrounding her to piece together her life story, so I could craft my cover before talking to her. First were the easy observations: she appeared to be about my age, but based on what I knew about the shifts at Adventure Alley, she was at the end of an overnight shift, meaning she was at least 18. Paying a bit more attention, I could see a backpack strap peeking out from behind the corner. The backpack paired with the fact that she worked the early Sunday morning shift told me she was likely a college student working her way through school.

Feeling the clock ticking, I quickly tried to find anything that might confirm my inference, or tell me what or where she was studying. As she set her novel down, paying more attention now that there was a customer in the store, I hit the jackpot. Setting her book down drew my attention to a textbook I had missed before.

I could just make out the title *Causes of Crime and Delinquency* on the spine of the textbook, and the pen slid into the spiral of the notebook she'd used as a bookmark boasted her admission into the Department of Sociology and Criminology at UNM.

Before she caught me staring at her, I returned my attention to the less than ideal breakfast options. I cursed myself for coming over here, because even starving, none of the options sounded appealing.

Man I was spoiled.

"If you're looking for something specific, I can see if we have it in the back," the cashier offered.

I looked up at her, smiling as I shook my head. "No, that's fine. Thanks though." I decided to give up trying to find something that looked appealing, and just approached the check-out counter. "I have lots of food in the car. I guess I was just hoping for something else, you know what I mean?" I asked her.

"The store food almost always sounds better than the stuff at home," the cashier agreed. "What can I help you with?"

"You know, I've been cooped up the car for too long. Is this location one of the ones with a shower?" I asked, as if I didn't know.

The cashier nodded. "All of our locations have showers. Would you like to purchase one?"

"Maybe," I replied. I knew that I wasn't going to, but I also knew that the Adventure Alley register would only display the prompt with the script for the cashier if there was a shower on the order when I gave her my rewards number. "Can you go ahead and ring me up for one?"

"Absolutely!" The smile she gave me screamed that she hadn't been in customer service for very long… or she loved her job. I sincerely doubted she enjoyed working the overnight shift at a convenience store and truck stop.

"How long have you worked here?" I asked. It was a super basic, normal question, but that just meant it was a good way to start a conversation with her to build the trust and rapport I needed to.

"A few months," she replied while finding the code for a shower.

I pointed at the textbook. "You going to school?"

She looked where I was pointing before nodding. Her face brightened. "Yeah. I'm studying Criminal Justice."

"That sounds awesome. Do you know what you want to do with your degree once you graduate?" Showing interest in a topic that the mark clearly enjoyed opened them up, and helped them feel connected. Based on the smile that resulted from my question, I was guessing I was on the correct track.

"Law Enforcement. My family has a legacy of service in Law Enforcement, and I was hoping to join them." She answered. "Do you have a rewards number you wanted to use?"

"Yes," I replied. "Whenever you're ready…"

"I'm ready," she smiled.

I took a deep breath, trying to imagine the alpha numeric keyboard to make sure I gave the cashier the correct phone number.

"4-2-5 7-8-6 2-4-0-1." I said. "My brother-in-law is actually training at Quantico for the FBI as we speak," I added while she finished typing in the number. Normally, I wouldn't opt such a blatant truth when using my training to build a connection, but the best covers were typically the ones that weaved pieces of truth in with the fabricated identity.

After making a similar safety fueled eastern drive just a few months ago, I knew the second the register displayed the message triggered by my phone number. I had watched the reactions of several cashiers in various states as Sarah had used the Adventure Alley network to safely get herself, Neil, Vee, and I from our safe-house in Northern California, to Neil's parents house in Virginia, and all of them had the same look of surprise and disbelief that the cashier helping me now had.

I guess it wasn't every day that they met a member of the owning family.

"It looks like you have a Premium Shower you can use, would you like to use that instead?" The cashier asked, glancing at the screen occasionally to ensure she used the right words.

"Actually, yeah, that would be great." I answered.

She nodded, selecting the correct option on the register, while I prepared for the security questions she would ask to make sure I was who I said I was. "What brings you to New Mexico?" She asked.

If I didn't know better I would think she was making small talk while she processed the order. The questions were innocent, unassuming questions that a normal cashier might ask. And I gave a normal answer that a normal customer might reply with. "Just traveling the country for my gap year. I had to see the iconic Route 66, you know?"

Her eyes stayed glued to the register, where I knew she was verifying my answer. Once she hit the enter key, verifying that I had answered within the parameters outlined, the register opened. Using the plastic walls dividing the various dominations of cash, she gripped the cash tray and lifted it, retrieving the key on the exclusive *Adventure Alley VIP* key chain.

"Enjoy your shower," she told me, handing me the key.

"I will thank you." I answered. I took a breath, securing the key in the palm of my hand. "Can I ask you a question about your degree?"

She nodded at me. "Sure."

"I'm just, trying to figure out what I want to do with my life, you know, and I looked at studying Criminal Justice…" I took a breath. I was fighting an internal battle to speak. Part of me was trying to say that my question would help me connect better with her. I knew it was an excuse. This was a personal question for no other purpose but my own improvement. "Is it worth it? Do you like it?"

"Absolutely!" She replied. I didn't hear any hesitation in her voice, and that said more than anything else. "Learning about the laws to enforce them is one thing, but learning why we have them, and why people break them makes a big difference."

I nodded. "Thanks for your help. I'm Emily, by the way."

She smiled. "Marie"

"Thank you, Marie," I said, now having her name.

"No problem," she smiled.

With a small awkward wave, I walked back towards the front door, trying to ignore the fact that I had just messed up.

Things were much easier when they didn't know your name.

07:40 MDT
Albuquerque, New Mexico
Adventure Alley Store 428

THERE WAS NO TRIUMPHANT RETURN when I returned with the key. The key wasn't held high. There were no cheers. I didn't expect loud celebration over my small accomplishment, but I also didn't expect Rafael to look… scared, anxious, angry? Guilty?

"Did you get the key?" He asked me when I was close enough he could speak softly and not be heard.

"Of course," I replied. I opened my hand so he could see it. "What's wrong?"

Rafael flinched. "I got a call while you were inside. They know I helped you. They know Ally asked me help you."

My stomach fell. "They who?"

Rafael gave me a meaningful look, telling me without words that I already knew.

And I did.

I didn't want it to be true, but I knew exactly who he meant. The Circle of Fifths knew. *Jackson* knew. Rafael may have just blown his cover coming to rescue me. I'd never met her, but he had a daughter waiting for him to come home.

"How?" My voice came out as a whispered whine. I was *so sick* of Jackson finding me, of discovering things in a timeframe that seemed impossible.

"I don't know," Rafael admitted.

He continued talking, but I wasn't really paying attention. While he mentioned something about splitting up, and flying back to Russia from New Mexico now, I was analyzing everything I had done since leaving LA the first time. It wasn't much, but I felt a small measure of safety standing by this gas pump on my family's property, so for the first time, I allowed myself to analyze everything I'd done wrong.

The problem was I couldn't identify what I'd done wrong. I'd switched cars before leaving LA. We paid cash at the gas station we stopped at just outside of Vegas. I parked the car in the garage, so even if Jackson had seen what car we switched to in LA, he didn't just stumble across the house.

More than that, Jackson attacked the safehouse before Ally had gotten off the plane. He got there no more than five and a half hours after we did. I knew he had to have driven to the Las Vegas safehouse from LA, because he somehow transported my unconscious body, and… I knew he had driven, so he had to have left LA at least five hours before he attacked us, which meant he knew where we were almost as soon as we set foot in the safehouse—

"…I'll call Ally. Do you remember the plan I laid out earlier?"

Rafael finished explaining whatever plan he'd been outlining for me while I disappeared into my head.

"You can't call Ally," I whispered. The answer for how everything had gone wrong was clearer to me now than anything had been before. The Circle of Fifths had Ally's phone records. I was certain of the fact; not even seeing the records in Jackson's possession would increase the certainty I felt.

It wasn't a coincidence that Jackson started driving to Las Vegas shortly after I made a call to Ally's cell phone from the safe house. If he'd used some bogus claim to access Ally's phone records, he would have seen the number show up, and Yellow Pages could tell him the address. No doubt, the same explanation could account for our current situation. I loved my sister, but with a secure international phone line, she probably didn't think twice about making the call to Rafael.

Heck, it wouldn't surprise me if Jackson suspected Rafael was on his way to rescue me when he'd left me alone. If he didn't, I'm sure the call I made from Rafael's phone to Ally immediately after I escaped told him what he needed.

"I need to update her on the change of plans. I promised her I would see that you got home safely. To protect you, I can't do that, and she deserves an explanation." Rafael insisted.

I nodded, "And she'll get one. But you can't just call her," I reiterated. "Listen, if you have been working for *them* for the last twelve years, clearly you know a thing or two about not getting caught, so why were you now?"

"I already told you I don't know. That's not the most pressing issue at the moment, Emily. Right now, the priority is getting you as far away from me as possible." Rafael argued.

"I thought I did something wrong , and that was why I was caught in Vegas." I continued my explanation as if he hadn't interrupted. "And while I don't have the experience you do, I couldn't figure out what it was. I did *everything* right. The only way Jackson could have found me was if it was *because* I followed procedure."

Rafael let out an exasperated sigh. "Emily, we don't have time—"

"The common denominator between you getting caught, and me getting caught, is we both called Ally," I finished.

"Your sister isn't a mole." The determination in Rafael's voice spoke to the trust she'd built with him, and I was grateful for it.

"I wasn't saying she is." I searched Rafael's face for any hint he knew where I was going with this. He didn't, so to save us from the tense silence, I continued: "Her phone has been compromised. My bet is Jackson created a bogus case, and pulled her records."

Rafael muttered a Russian word I recognized as a swear. "Someone has to tell her."

I knew what he meant. Someone would have to call Ally and let her know her phone was compromised, otherwise, whoever she called or called her would also be compromised. I had already started running through our options:

If I called her, the Circle of Fifths would know I was in Albuquerque.

If Rafael called her immediately after they called him, he would blow his cover, if it hadn't been already.

Michael was automatically ruled out because his phone was likely compromised as well.

I could call Sarah, but if the Circle of Fifths got ahold of her number, they'd know she was in Virginia, and she'd have to drop out of nursing school to take Vee on the run… again.

Hypothetically, Dylan was an option. He changed numbers and locations regularly, and when he could, he relayed sensitive information in person. The problem with him was I would have to leave a coded message for him. If he'd already checked his messages today, he wouldn't get it until tomorrow, at which point he'd arrange travel to go see Ally. In the meantime, who knows how many calls Ally would make.

My least favorite option also happened to objectively be the best: Call my mom. Did I want my mom knowing I had ditched school to play spy and fail? Absolutely not. If I called her, she would no doubt lecture me about the importance of not operating way beyond my abilities. But at the end of the lecture, I knew she'd tell me she loved me, then relay my message to Ally without putting herself in any unnecessary danger.

By the time I arrived at my next stop, all of my siblings would be safely notified of the breach, and I would have a message with Ally's new number waiting for me.

So despite the pit in my stomach just anticipating having to make the call, I looked at Rafael and told him, "I'll call my mom."

I watched Rafael as he processed my decision, and came to the same conclusion as I had.

"You should return the rental, and book a flight home. I'll make the call. Ally should get my message, and call you from a secure phone before your flight boards." As I was walking through my new plan, I knew it was the only option. "I know the way to Virginia. I can make the drive by myself."

"How will you check in?" Rafael asked.

I pointed towards the store. "I already have. When I got the key, I used my unique number. Anyone in the family with access can track my progress."

Rafael nodded, opening his car door. "I probably won't see you again for a while. Be careful."

"I will," I promised.

How many times in the last few days had I made that same promise. I meant it every time I made it, but I had found myself in more trouble than I could feasibly escape every time I'd made that promise.

I could only hope the same wasn't true this time.

07:55 MDT
Albuquerque, New Mexico
Adventure Alley Store 428

"ALLÔ?" IT WAS A SIMPLE, customary French phone greeting, but hearing it when the line connected caused my stomach to bind with the nerves I'd been suppressing to make the call.

I'd taken my time changing my clothes, but I hadn't been able to put off calling my mother any longer. As much as I would have loved a shower to wash the days of running and captivity off of me, as soon as Rafael returned the car and bought a plane ticket, the Circle of Fifths would know the general vicinity he split ways from me. I was racing against the clock to make sure I stayed ahead of Jackson.

I needed to be as quick as I could on this call so I could get back on the road.

"Maman, c'est Emily." I answered my mother in French, as I always had growing up.

My mom spoke English, but her first language had been French, and she'd insisted my siblings and I learn French with English. At school, I may have selected English as my native language, but that was just because they wouldn't let me select two.

It had been a while since I'd been in a home that regularly spoke French, but as my mom began speaking, it felt like it'd been no time at all since I was that twelve-year-old girl speaking English with my father, and French with *ma mère.*

"Emily Nour Hall, why are you calling me from Adventure Alley 428?" Her French was fast, and aggressive. If I hadn't grown up speaking French, I probably wouldn't understand any of this conversation.

"Because I needed to change cars and clothes," I replied.

"Don't be smart with me," she chastised.

"I was helping Ally with something. It didn't go well. I'm heading back to the McLean's. I'm calling because her phone has been compromised, and I need someone to let her know before anyone else is compromised," I explained.

"Who is chasing you?" My mom asked.

"Maman…"

"Emily…" my mom mimicked. "Who compromised your sister's phone? How much danger are my children in?"

Hearing my mom refer to my siblings and I as *mes enfants* had me wanting to argue with her, but I knew that the impulse was coming from the English side of my brain. *That word sounded too much like infant.*

"A man named Phil Jackson. He works for the Circle of Fifths," I conceded. I hadn't wanted to tell my mom that Ally and I had been going after the Circle of Fifths. Since my dad died, she had been against any of her children chasing the terrorists.

She didn't want any of her children to die at the same hands as our father.

"We extracted his sister and her family. I sent Ally home, and I drove his sister to Lamb Park, but he found us. The only way that makes sense is if he saw the phone number show up on Ally's phone records." If I was going to tell my mom that we'd been chasing the Circle of Fifths, I might as well tell her the entire story so her lecture was accurate.

"Get home as soon as you can, and call me. If I don't hear from you by Tuesday morning, I'm calling Madelyn."

I didn't realize Neil's mother scared me until my mom threatened to call her. If I hadn't already been anxious to get home, I was now. "Maman," I whispered quietly, "they were on Sarah's team. Even when we didn't go after them, they came after us. They attacked Sarah's children to hurt her."

My mom was silent on the other side of the phone, probably mulling over what I'd said. I think she always assumed that if the Hall family stopped chasing the Circle of Fifths, they would stop attacking us.

The fact that they hadn't told me that they were terrified of us. We threatened their organization more than we realized.

"Emily, sois prudent. Je t'aime." My mother said.

"Je t'aime aussi," I replied.

Before I knew it, I'd returned the safehouse key to the cashier, and was climbing into the beige interior of the dark green Honda Accord EX that had been stored in the garage. I opened the glove-box to see what CDs had been stashed for the drive, finding Def Leppard's *Hysteria*, *Marching to Mars* by Sammy Hagar, The *Top Gun* soundtrack, and some 80s Rock compilation CD.

I turned on the car, grabbed the red *Marching to Mars* CD from its case, and fed the CD into the player. With the CDs opening track "Little White Lies" playing from the stereo, I followed the signs towards east bound I-40 and merged with traffic. I put on the sunglasses I'd grabbed from the safehouse to protect my eyes from the rising sun, turned up the music, and set the cruise control to 5 miles per hour over the speed limit—fast enough to keep up with the flow of traffic, but not so fast I'd get pulled over.

I was driving the second most popular car in the US, in the 4th most popular color, at the average speed of the surrounding drivers. I was just your average driver on any average morning.

Totally forgettable, just the way I liked it.

08:15 MDT
Albuquerque, New Mexico
ABQ International Sunport Rental Return

RAFAEL HAD ALWAYS PRIDED HIMSELF on his ability to blend into his surroundings. He had developed enough of a knowledge of men's fashion around the world that wherever he went, he could tailor his style to match the locals. However, as he stepped out of the Rental Car returns office, he was reminded how much fashion changed from state to state in America. The same smart business casual that had helped him blend in when he arrived in LA would have also worked in Virginia where he planned to fly home. But in New Mexico, his navy blazer over a light blue polo shirt tucked into gray slacks, with a matching conservative brown leather belt, loafers, and messenger bag made him stick out among the Native American inspired geometric patterns, bolo ties, and turquoise jewelry popular in New Mexico fashion.

Despite feeling out of place, Rafael walked away from the rental car return with confidence. If he convinced himself he belonged here, he could convince those around him that he belonged here.

As he walked towards the terminal, he heard his phone ring.

He pulled the titanium Motorola Razr from his right front pocket, flicking it open to answer it.

He expected Ally to call him as soon as Emily's message had reached her, but he hadn't expected it to be quite so soon.

"Rafael Feilds," he said in greeting once he had the phone up to his ear.

One thing he'd learned over the years, was to never assume who was calling, even when he was expecting a call.

"What happened?" Ally asked.

Rafael grimaced as he walked through the sliding glass doors of the terminal. "Jackson happened. He knows I helped you. He knows I helped Emily. Now he wants proof of my dedication to the *cause*."

"Where are you now?" Ally asked.

"The airport. I'm flying home," Rafael answered, using the signs above him to find the line for a booking agent.

"What about Emily?" Ally asked in a panic.

"She's on her way home, just as you'd planned," Rafael answered.

"No, the plan was to have you take her home. Jackson is after her, and she's not strong enough—"

Rafael interrupted his sister-in-law, correcting the woman who was rarely wrong. "Jackson is after *you*, and your sister is more capable than you are giving her credit for. I didn't rescue Emily, she rescued herself. It was a matter of divine timing I got there when I did to begin driving her home. Not to mention she was only captured in the first place because she called *you*, and she's the one who figured that out. *Your* phone was compromised; *your* involvement is the reason she failed."

"I'm the reason a little boy is in danger," Ally breathed.

"Little boy?" Rafael asked, getting in line behind a woman with a very ornate silver and turquoise bracelet. With more time in New Mexico, he might buy some jewelry for his wife, or maybe even his daughter. His wife's jewelry preference leaned toward the intricate filigree common in Imperial Russian jewelry, typically with deep blue sapphires, or rich green emeralds. As he glanced around the airport at the the turquoise jewelry, he recognized the intricacies in the silver smithing his wife preferred, and the rich color of the turquoise stones reminded him of his wife's favorite colors.

Ally's voice through his phone dragged him back to reality, and why he couldn't drive around New Mexico to find his wife a present. "Emily was protecting Jackson's sister and her family, including her seven-year-old little boy. Jackson killed his sister and her husband, and kidnapped Kalen, their son."

Rafael couldn't help but close his eyes and see his daughter's face. Lyshiria was seven. She was the light of his life; she exuded innocence and grace. He would do just about anything to protect her. It didn't surprise him that Kalen's parents had died trying to protect him.

"You said Jackson wants proof of your dedication to the cause. What did he ask you to do?" Ally asked after a moment of silence.

Rafael sighed. "Give him you."

TOP SECRET PROMISING GENERATION EYES ONLY

Operation Subversion
Objective: Systematically dismantle the Circle of Fifths

FIELD REPORT:23 October 2000

CLASSIFIED TOP SECRET

17:58 EDT McLean Residence; McLean, VA

17:58 EDT
McLean, Virginia
McLean Residence

KNOCKING ON THE DOOR OF the house I'd been living in the past few months felt weird. I don't know when it had started to feel like home, but I felt an overwhelming sense of peace and security waiting on the other side of the door. After everything that had happened, I craved that feeling, but instead of walking in the front door like I belonged here, I stood on the porch like an outsider waiting to be granted asylum.

My heart rate quickened as I heard the door unlock. I watched as the door opened and I came face to face with my sister. Logically, I knew it was Sarah; she was the one who was living here, but I couldn't help but hope Ally was here too.

While I stood frozen on the porch, feeling unworthy of the safety inside, Sarah pulled me into a bone-crushing hug. "I was worried sick," Sarah admitted. "Ally said you were helping her with something, then mom called and told me that you called her from an Adventure Alley, and Ally's phone had been compromised, so I couldn't call Ally to ask her what happened…"

"I'm fine, just a little sore from driving," I told Sarah.

Sarah pulled away from me, giving me a look that screamed her disbelief. "Someone who's *fine* doesn't use the Adventure Alleys."

"I'm tired, and I need to call maman. Can we argue about this later?" I asked, rubbing my face with my hand.

Before I could stop her, Sarah had grabbed my arm, and was gently examining my wrist, which was still bruised from being tied up with power cords, before making eye contact with me.

I couldn't lie. She knew. She recognized the bruises.

She released my arm, putting her arm around me instead to bring me into the house. She pushed me upstairs to the room she was supposed to share with Neil, if either of them ever stayed in the house longer than the few minutes it took to change clothes and say hi to Vee. She sat me down on the bed and pulled out a first aid kit that was much bigger than one you'd typically find in a house.

"Sarah, I promised I'd call maman and let her know I arrived safely," I argued. Did I want to call my mom? Not really. I knew she had a lengthy lecture prepared for me, but right now, a lecture sounded more enjoyable than Sarah cleaning the broken skin on my wrists. I had barely managed to clean the dried blood off of them with soap and water in Albuquerque, and the hot water of the shower in Arkansas had made them sting enough I hadn't even attempted to clean my ankles, which looked even worse, considering my shuffle to get the scissors and cut myself free had rubbed them raw. If Sarah got out the hydrogen peroxide…

Sure enough, the small brown bottle made its way out of the first aid kit. As Sarah grabbed a cotton ball, and opened the bottle, I squirmed. “Really, my wrists are fine. They barely even hurt. I already cleaned them. They won’t get infected, I promise.”

“No, they won’t get infected, because you are going to tell me what you were helping Ally with, and why you were tied up while I clean and bandage your wrists.” The way Sarah spoke, I knew it was prudent to listen to her and do what she said.

I was beginning to understand her reputation in the CIA.

“Ally discovered evidence that the Circle of Fifths had someone on your team in California, someone imbedded in the Promising Generation. She needed my help to figure out who. I figured it out, and even turned two of them into assets,” I started.

“These aren’t wounds of a victor,” Sarah commented.

I sighed, “No. One of the members of the Circle of Fifths I turned was compromised. Ally and I tried to pull her out, and things went wrong. I took the family to Lamb Park, but Ally’s phone was compromised, so checking in meant we got caught. I’m sure you can figure out the rest.”

Sarah didn’t say anything as she applied an antibiotic cream to my wrists before wrapping them with a soft gauze.

I wasn’t sure if I should be glad she didn’t say anything about my story, or scared.

“Let me see your ankles,” Sarah said as she finished taking care of my wrists.

I started to panic. My ankles were most definitely worse than my wrists. I don't think I'd been able to fully clean them yet. I knew I needed to, and I should be glad that Sarah could take care of something I hadn't been able to, but it also meant giving up control.

"Why do you want to see my ankles?" I asked, trying to hide my fear of showing her.

Sarah didn't answer, simply placing her hand under my calf lifting one of my legs up onto her lap where she took off my shoe and sock, then rolled up the cuff of my pants.

I hadn't spent too long looking at my ankles, but I knew they didn't look great. Based on the concern I saw on Sarah's face, they were pretty bad.

If she wanted to be a good nurse, she was going to have to work on her poker face.

"That good, huh?" I asked sarcastically.

Sarah looked up at me; her lips were tightly pressed together as she took a deep breath through her nose, something she typically did to remain calm. "Did you try to clean these?"

"Kinda. It hurt enough I kept flinching away from it, so I know it's not perfect." I admitted.

"Not perfect?! Emily, this—" Sarah stopped herself, pressing her lips together again to take another deep breath.

Sarah got up, walking over to the dresser that sat on the wall across from the bed. She opened the middle drawer on the right hand side, pulling out a pair of sweat shorts.

She tossed the shorts at me. "Put those on," she ordered before walking into the attached bathroom, where I heard her start the bath.

I knew Sarah was trying not to get mad at me, and I didn't want to give her any excuse to yell, so I did as she asked, took off my other shoe, and put on the shorts.

And it hurt.

As the coarse material of the jeans slid over the bruises on my ankles, I had a swallow a whimper, and pulling on the sweat shorts wasn't much better.

By the time Sarah came back into the room, I'd somehow managed to change into the shorts she'd given me. I'd even taken off the sock Sarah hadn't, mostly because it was weird to only have one on, but also because I figured she would appreciate it.

Sarah glanced to make sure I'd done as I'd been told, then gestured for me to follow her into the bathroom. When I walked through the door, she pointed at the side of the tub and said, "Sit."

So I did.

Sarah lifted both of my feet and placed them into the five inches of water that filled the tub.

I hissed as the water stung the cuts, trying my best to control the instinct to remove my feet from the tub. Unfortunately in the battle of will versus flinch, I almost always lost; I jerked my feet back out of the water, losing my balance while I was at it.

Sarah caught me, preventing me from hitting my head and sustaining further injury. "Emily," she scolded. "I know it hurts, but I need you to let me do my job and clean the cuts. There is so much dried blood on these I can't tell if they are infected or not."

I nodded, taking a deep breath to prepare myself for the stinging I'd feel once Sarah put my feet back in the water.

This time when she submerged my feet in the water again, I was prepared for the pain of the water hitting the open cuts. It was almost like the initial shock had worn off, and now I was able to ignore it and not flinch.

The problem was, Sarah was wetting a washcloth, adding the slightest bit of soap to it, and I was terrified I wouldn't be able to hold still as she tried to run the rough cloth across the cuts to clean them.

"Mommy, mommy!" The small voice of Vee came echoing through the open door connecting the bathroom to Sarah and Neil's room. "Grandma said that the doorbell was Emily, but I can't find…"

Vee trailed off as she entered the room and saw me sitting on the side of the tub. Her face lit up, and she took off running at me.

"Emily!" She yelled, throwing herself at me. I twisted around so I could catch her for the hug I knew she wanted. "You're back. I thought you'd be gone *forever*. It took you so long to come back."

"I'm sorry, Vee. I didn't mean to stay away for so long," I apologized.

Vee shrugged. "It's ok. You're back now, which means I can show you what I made at school today."

Vee grabbed my hand, trying to pull me from my seat on the bathtub.

"Hold up, Bug. I need to clean Em's cuts." Sarah told Vee.

Vee turned and looked at me a bit closer than she had before. She ran her fingers over the gauze that covered my wrists, then leaned over to peek at my feet in the bathtub. "Owie," she commented.

"Yeah, owie," Sarah replied. "Would you do me a favor? Can you sit with Emily and hold her hand? She's trying to be strong, but she could use your support while I clean her cuts so they don't get infected."

Vee nodded her head, letting go of my hand so she could climb up and sit in my lap. I wrapped my arms around her so she wouldn't fall and hit her head.

When Sarah grabbed my left ankle, lifting it out of the water to begin cleaning it, I felt the tears welling in my eyes, but not just from the pain. After the last several days, and the several successes and failures I'd lived through, it was so nice to be reminded why I'd left with Ally in the first place.

"Emily, are you going to drive me to school tomorrow?" Vee asked me.

I had my eyes tightly closed, trying to block out the pain so I didn't squeeze Vee too tight, when she asked the question. I could feel her playing with the strands of my hair that had fallen out of the braid I'd put my hair in after my shower in Arkansas. All of those small things distracted me enough I didn't have a reply faster than Sarah, and the words that came out of her mouth reminded me she was still mad at me.

"Of course she will. Has there been a day where she went to school and didn't drive you?" Sarah asked her daughter.

Vee bounced in my lap. "Really? I mean, I love Grandma McLean, and it was nice to have her drop me off, but it wasn't the same as going to school with you," Vee told me. It had been a while since I had seen her this excited about something.

I glanced at Sarah. I'd never told her I was planning on going to school tomorrow. In fact, after the last few days I'd had, I was planning on taking another day off to catch up on the assignments I'd missed, and recover from the beating I'd put my body through. She looked like she was focused on cleaning my ankle, but I could see the slightest smirk on her face.

Sarah knew I'd been planning on staying home another day, and she was using Vee to make sure I didn't.

And it was working. How could I disappoint Vee when she was so excited about something so small?

I made a mental note, adding *catch up on homework*, to my list of things to do after calling my mom.

TOP SECRET PROMISING GENERATION EYES ONLY

Operation Subversion
Objective: Systematically dismantle the Circle of Fifths

FIELD REPORT: 24 October 2000

CLASSIFIED TOP SECRET

07:05 EDT McLean Residence; McLean, VA
14:12 MSD Skazka Kafe; Moscow, Russia
15:10 EDT Potomac School; McLean, VA
15:38 EDT McLean Residence; McLean, VA

Tuesday

07:05 EDT
McLean, Virginia
McLean Residence

THE PSYCHOLOGY CLASS I'D TAKEN in California had an entire unit on sleep. It had been one of my favorite classes, for several reasons, at least half of them relating to my chosen future profession, so I paid attention to every unit, even if I didn't think it would be applicable.

As I wandered down the stairs after getting maybe 3 hours of sleep, the chapter about sleep depravation and its effects scrolled through my mind. They recommended that teenagers get between 8 and 10 hours of sleep a night, and I was lucky if I'd gotten an *average* of 6 hours of sleep a night over the last week. That was counting the unconscious stints, and I wasn't sure if that really counted.

I walked into the kitchen, chucking my backpack onto the floor before sliding onto a stool. Sarah sat at the end of the kitchen island, acting like a doting mother by running her hand over Vee's hair while the five-year-old ate the breakfast Madelyn had prepared. I didn't need to look at my sister to see her smirking into her glass of Orange juice.

"You get your homework done?" Sarah asked.

I just turned my head and glared at her. *Of course* I got my homework done. That was the reason I was exhausted. Then, because she liked to annoy me, Sarah had woken me up at 6 am to check my wounds before sending me to shower, then redressing them with gauze.

It hadn't mattered how much I'd argued against the gauze dressings, Sarah had insisted it was the best way to ensure they didn't get infected. The ankle dressings I had been able to hide with the uniform socks, as uncomfortable that was, but the dressings on my wrists were harder.

Much harder.

Usually, I was able to get up at 6:30, and I was dressed and ready by 6:45 when I'd get Vee up to start getting her ready for school. Instead, I'd spent half an hour trying to find one of my uniforms that would hide the gauze on my wrists.

My classmates already had enough to talk about. I didn't need them speculating about the gauze on my wrists after missing three days of school. I could already hear the stories they'd come up with.

"Right now, your job is to go to school," Sarah commented, making eye contact with me. "You shouldn't be out playing spy."

"Oh, so it's ok for you to ask me to play mother to your child, but Ally can't ask me for my help with something that I've been training for *since I was five*?" I retorted. "Let's not forget who trained me, because it wasn't just Ally."

"I never asked you to play mother," Sarah replied.

"No," I admitted, "you just moved across the country, dumped her at your in-law's house, pushed your husband away, then disappeared. I get she reminds you of what you lost, but it's not her fault she survived."

"Perhaps now is not the time for this conversation," Madelyn commented, putting food in front of me. "You need to eat before going to school, not argue with your sister about her unhealthy coping mechanisms."

"What coping mechanisms are unhealthy?" Sarah asked.

Madelyn gave Sarah a look that asked *really?* "If you truly don't know what I'm talking about, we can discuss it once the girls leave for school, assuming you will stick around long enough."

Suddenly, I was understanding why the thought of my mom calling Madelyn scared me. She was extremely kind and caring, but that was by no means a sign of weakness.

She could be downright terrifying when the situation called for it.

I shoved food in my mouth to prevent myself from continuing the argument with Sarah. It would be best if I did what Madelyn asked and ate my food before driving Vee and I to school.

14:12 MSD (GMT +4)
Moscow, Russia
Skazka Kafe

ALLY TOOK SMALL SIPS OF her water as she pretended to read the menu, when what she was really doing was keeping a close eye on the door. She couldn't help but feel as though she was at a major disadvantage. She loved Michael, and wouldn't sacrifice her relationship with him for anything in the world, but their marriage came with some annoying consequences.

Like her face being splashed across the front page of tabloids.

It had been a big adjustment, not just for her, but for Sarah as well, when Ally had decided she was serious about Michael. Ally had been able to maintain her privacy and anonymity while hers and Michael's relationship consisted of long distance letter writing and covert rendezvous, but when they decided they actually wanted to get married, both Ally and Sarah had to give up their dreams of a career in covert ops. They couldn't blend into the crowd when the crowd recognized their face from the front of Britain's tabloids.

It was also difficult to take on the persona of someone else, when most of the world knew your name.

When it came to meets like this one, Ally felt exposed. She knew nothing about what Jackson looked like. If she was lucky, he would share some features with his sister, and Ally could use those features to identify the killer among the restaurant patrons, but the moment Jackson entered the establishment, he could use the tabloids to identify her.

Since Jackson was walking in with an advantage she couldn't control, she stole any advantage she could. The meet had been scheduled for 1430; she showed up at 1400. She knew her early arrival would afford her the choice of choosing the table, and as much as it pained her to go against a lifetime of training, she chose a table that did just that.

She had strategically selected a table that was centrally located; the surrounding tables had other patrons dining close enough they could listen in if they so desired and the staff passed by the table frequently. Usually, a table like this one would be the first she eliminated as a possibility.

Usually, she was meeting someone she trusted…with backup.

Fortunately, the table was orientated so one chair faced the door while the other faced away, so Ally had placed herself in the chair facing the door.

Over the top of her menu, she caught sight of a man entering the restaurant. Something about him screamed danger, but Ally couldn't study him without endangering Rafael's cover. After all, she was meant to believe she was meeting Rafael to discuss his *payment* for rescuing Emily. She wasn't supposed to know Jackson was coming instead.

Using her peripheral vision, she kept tabs on the new man. He was 15 minutes early, but when he almost immediately began to make his way toward Ally, she knew this was the man that had killed two people, then kidnapped Emily and Kalen.

It was time. Whether she was ready or not, the chess match had begun. Her acting skills needed to be flawless, or she would be endangering more than just her own life.

She knew the easiest way to ensure Rafael's cover remained in tact, and Jackson remained oblivious to this set-up was for her to act surprised when he approached her. The tricky part wasn't faking the surprise, it was making sure she hid it just well enough it seemed real, but not so well that Jackson didn't catch it.

If she did this right, Jackson would believe what Rafael had told him: Ally Feilds didn't trust anyone, not even her own brother-in law.

Jackson sat down in the chair across the table from Ally. She looked up, feigning a brief moment of surprise that she then hid before speaking. "I'm sorry, but I am waiting for someone," she said in Russian.

If Jackson's smile said anything, it seemed he bought her surprise. Rafael's cover was intact.

Thank Sarah for the acting lessons.

"I know. Rafael is very sorry he couldn't make it, but I came to discuss his payment on his behalf," Jackson replied. His Russian was decent, but it wasn't good enough to help him pass as a native.

Whether or not that was his goal, Ally had no idea. It was also hard to care, when hearing his voice was the final confirmation she needed. This was most definitely the man who had kidnapped her sister. Ally may not have seen Emily herself, but based on what Rafael and Sarah reported, Jackson hadn't left Emily unscathed.

Without even having to act, Ally felt her jaw tighten, revealing the anger she felt towards the man who had hurt her sister.

And seeing her anger, the man had the audacity to *smirk*.

Ally took a deep breath, releasing the tension from her body to appear as the cool, calm spy she was supposed to be. "And what, may I ask, do you get from negotiating on Rafael's behalf?" Ally asked.

"The payment," Jackson replied.

The hairs on the back of Ally's neck stood up. She had a good idea of what payment Jackson was expecting. She had come to the meet knowing that Jackson would be here, and that he was after her. But something about the way he spoke—something about the way he didn't seem perturbed by her choice in seating—unnerved her.

He was acting like a man whose victory was assured.

Despite already knowing the answer, Ally still asked the question: "And what payment are you hoping for?"

Jackson smiled, leaning across the table. "The same payment I outlined when I caught your sister. You saved your sister's life. It's time to give me yours."

15:10 EDT
McLean, Virginia
Upper School, Potomac School

BY THE TIME THE FINAL bell of the day rang, I was having a hard time staying awake. I was on autopilot as I walked out of the classroom, against the flow of bodies in the hall, to the lower school playground. I was barely coherent enough to notice the increased stares and whispers, probably the result of whatever rumors had been spread to explain the *new girl's* absence.

As I pushed my way out of the upper school building, I dug through the front pocket of my backpack to find my new Nokia and turn it on. Apparently after taking off to California and getting myself kidnapped, Sarah wanted me to text her when I was leaving school. I was happy she wanted to be a more involved guardian, but I wasn't happy it meant she wanted to micromanage my life.

Then again, Sarah hadn't been very happy about driving to the phone store to get me a new phone last night. She may have understood why I'd ditched it in LA before driving Kyrie and her family to the safehouse, but I wasn't old enough to sign my own phone contract, which meant that responsibility fell on Sarah.

No matter how annoying I thought her new request was, I had to do it, because she was paying for my phone.

As my phone came back on, it began buzzing incessantly, alerting me to the numerous calls I'd missed while my phone was off. Before I had a chance to look at my missed calls, it began to buzz again. Looking at the number on the screen, it wasn't one I recognized, but curiosity won, leading me to hit the green phone button, and put the phone up to my ear saying, "Hello?"

"Emily, thank goodness. I've been trying to reach you for hours."

I may not have spent very much time with Rafael, but I recognized his voice. I took my phone away from my ear. Sure enough, I saw the +7 indicating the number originated from Russia.

"I was at school and my phone was off. How did you get my number?" I asked. I knew there were probably more pressing questions, but my fatigue was making it hard to focus, and the question felt so big in my head, I couldn't focus on anything else until I asked it and got an answer.

I desperately needed to go home and sleep.

"Ally gave it to me when she asked me to help you in California. But that's not important right now. Have you heard from Ally?" Rafael asked, redirecting my brain to the more important questions.

"Not since I got home. She talked to Sarah last night though." I replied.

When the next word I heard through the phone was a Russian swear word, my thoughts of sleep disappeared.

"What's wrong?" I whispered.

My tired brain was suddenly swimming with a myriad of reasons Rafael would be swearing about me not hearing from my sister, and none of them were good. It took me longer than it might have with proper sleep, but I knew my sister. As soon as she knew I was ok she likely enacted a plan to ensure Jackson wouldn't come after me again.

Before Rafael could answer my whispered question, I knew why he was hoping I'd heard from her. "She tried to do something about Jackson, didn't she?"

Rafael sighed on the other end. "Jackson wanted me to prove my loyalty to the Circle of Fifths. He asked me to set up a meet with your sister that he could crash. I told her what he wanted me to do, and she insisted I go through with it. She said it would be a good opportunity to get Kalen back while he was focused on her."

"And did you?" I asked, then realized I wasn't clear what I was asking, so I added, "Get Kalen back?"

"No. The intel your sister collected suggested he would be in London, but he wasn't. I wouldn't be surprised if he never left California." Rafael told me. "Your sister was supposed to meet with Jackson in Moscow at 1430 local time. She was supposed to call me an hour after that."

"Moscow is how many hours ahead of Greenwich Mean Time? Three?" I asked, trying to do the mental calculations to figure out how long ago Ally was supposed to call.

"Four," Rafael answered. "She should have called almost seven hours ago."

I wasn't sure why I had been trying to do the math to figure out how long ago she was supposed to call Rafael. She was late for a call-in. Whether she was late by an hour or seven, it meant the same thing.

The only way Ally would be late for a call-in was if she was physically incapable of making the call, or sending a text saying she'd be late.

Ally had either been kidnapped or killed. And since the Circle of Fifths didn't take prisoners…

With each stride that took me closer to the lower school playground, I tried to come up with a plausible explanation for why Ally hadn't called, but for every step that brought me an idea, the next reminded me why that idea couldn't be the reason she hadn't called.

"Emily?" Rafael asked, probably checking to make sure I was still on the line since I'd gone silent.

"Does anyone else know?" I asked quietly.

Rafael sighed. "No. Ally didn't want anyone else to know. She didn't want to risk my cover. Unfortunately, that also means I didn't have anyone else to call."

That meant no one was looking for her. No one knew where to start looking.

"She was supposed to go home after the meet, so Michael

should be expecting her to come home. When she doesn't he will raise the alarm, I'm sure," Rafael added.

I knew Rafael was right. The problem was it was already too late.

15:38 EDT
McLean, Virginia
McLean Residence

WHEN WE WALKED THROUGH THE front door of the McLean's house, it felt like Vee and I had switched places. For the first time in a while, Vee was still excited when we got home, and she was trying to use her good mood to improve my rather lackluster one. If I wasn't stuck in my head, trying to come up with ways I could convince Madelyn and Sarah to let me go to Russia and start looking for Ally, Vee probably would have succeeded.

Tired of my moodiness, Vee ran inside the house as soon as I unlocked and opened the door. Her footsteps echoed through the kitchen and into the family room. If I had to guess, she was running to the stairs that would take her to the basement where there was a library, probably because that was where Madelyn usually was this time of day. I didn't need to use my training to know what she was thinking: I was being boring, so she was going to find someone who would be excited about what she had to say.

Sure enough, as I rounded the corner into the kitchen, I watched as Vee opened the door that took her to the basement stairs. Instead of following Vee, I cut between the kitchen and family room, and headed for the stairs that would take me upstairs. With the amount of energy Vee had, she could keep Madelyn distracted long enough for me to pack a bag and sneak out. I knew it didn't make sense for me to hop on a plane to Moscow to look for my sister. By the time I arrived, too much time would have already passed, but I couldn't sit in this house, go to school, and pretend like nothing was wrong.

It had already been hard enough to sit in a classroom pretending to care about the fictional problems of a fictional 18th century character when I knew there was a seven-year-old boy living through his own personal hell. How could I go to school and pretend like the world was fine when my attempts to take down a terrorist organization had resulted in the torture or death of my own sister?

I had almost made it to the stairs when I heard a voice I wasn't expecting call my name. If it had been anyone else, I probably would have pretended I didn't hear him, and continue on my way up the stairs. But when I heard Deputy Director McLean call me, I froze. He was never home at this time of day. If he was home, and was asking to talk to me…

I dumped my backpack on the stairs in protest, but walked back the way I'd come. I knew I'd heard his voice come from the back part of the house, and while I was far enough away I couldn't pin point exactly where he was, I knew he had an office just off of the family room. That was where logic told me he was, so that's where I went.

Walking into the office, I knew I was right; when I saw Sarah sitting in one of the guest chairs, discreetly trying to wipe away tears, I also knew that Ally's absence had been noticed.

I should have been relieved. If they knew, that meant Michael knew, and people were looking for Ally. Instead, the pit that had settled in my stomach with Rafael's phone call turned into nausea. I could guess why they wanted to talk to me, and if I was right…

Deputy Director McLean looked at me with a stern face, then asked me the last question I wanted him to ask: "How did you get to Albuquerque?"

They were looking for the wrong man.

TOP SECRET PROMISING GENERATION EYES ONLY

Operation Subversion
Objective: Systematically dismantle the Circle of Fifths

FIELD REPORT:25 October 2000

CLASSIFIED TOP SECRET

03:16 MSD Unlisted Black site; Moscow, Russia

03:16 MSD
Moscow, Russia
Unlisted Blacksite

CONSCIOUSNESS CAME BACK SLOWLY. As feeling returned, the dream Ally had been having slowly faded. Her body hurt, but not in the way she had become accustomed to during her pregnancy. This wasn't just a slight discomfort caused by her body changing to support the growing life inside her.

She wanted to take a deep breath, but didn't want the change in breathing to alert whoever might be in the room with her. Instead, she used the meditation techniques she had learned to take stock of her situation. She started at the top of her head, slowly going down her body, cataloguing her pain.

There was a tugging pain starting in her neck and stretching down her back. There was a dull ache in her shoulders. Something hard was digging into her upper arms, causing pain there and tingling in her hands. Her butt was numb, a feeling she got when she sat on something hard for too long. Her knees were stiff from being bent too long.

Ally listened to what her body was trying to tell her, and without having to open her eyes, she had a clear picture of where she was: She was tied to a chair. And based on the way an unnatural chill leeched into her anywhere her body touched it, it was a metal one.

Now that she knew where she was, Ally started to go through her memory to try and figure out how she might have ended up here. She remembered the cafe, and meeting Jackson, and the confidence he had, despite everything she had done to protect herself against him. But after that, it was just blank.

How did he get her? And how long ago was that?

Before she was able to search her memory for how Jackson had caught her, or use her senses to figure out how long she'd been here, she felt someone come close to her. She could feel the change in the heat of the air around her as she heard footsteps stop close by. The pressure to ensure her breathing remained the same to not give off any signs that she was awake increased for one very important reason: she needed time.

She needed time to identify her limits. She needed time to identify any opportunities she might have to escape. Most importantly, once she'd done the first two, she needed time to come up with a plan. She knew that once Jackson found out she was awake, that time would be gone.

She didn't know what Jackson planned on doing with her, but she knew it was nothing good.

Unfortunately, while keeping her breathing nice and even, she failed to prepare herself for the possibility that the person walking around her might touch her. As two cold fingers pressed into the soft skin next to her windpipe, presumably to check her pulse, she flinched.

"She's waking up," a deep voice said from above her.

"Pull her up," Jackson ordered.

The next thing Ally knew, the rope that tied her wrists together wrenched her shoulders up at an unnatural, and very painful, angle. The scream that tore from her mouth was involuntary, and ruined all previous pretense of sleep.

With eyes now open, Ally decided now was a good time to try to observe her surroundings and try to identify possible escape routes. The problem was the rope kept pulling her arms up, and her shoulders had already reached their limits for mobility. She wasn't tied to the chair anywhere else, so first, her torso angled forward limiting how far she could look around. She forgot about her mission to look around when her body started lifting from the chair, putting all her weight on her unnaturally bent arms.

"I learned something quite useful while I had your sister," Jackson said.

Ally could hear him much closer to her than he had been before. She tried to remain calm. He wanted her on edge. He wanted her angry. He wanted her scared.

She couldn't give him what he wanted.

"That girl is quite determined. Doesn't know when to give up. Even when I had my arm around her neck, and literally held her life in my hands, she refused to answer my questions," Jackson complained.

Ally closed her eyes, picturing one of her favorite moments of her life thus far: Michael holding a newborn Kate for the first time. She basked in the love she'd felt for her husband and new child at that moment in order to counteract the anger that started building with Jackson's description.

"For the 32 hours she was my captive, she was conscious and in my presence for 18. Out of all the CIA interrogators authorized to used enhanced interrogation, I am the most effective. I produce more results than anyone else, and faster. Yet, for those 18 hours, she remained defiant."

Ally took a deep breath, remembering the joy she felt when she helped Kate take her first steps, then watched with love as her awkward steps took her to Michael, who picked her up with a huge smile and spun her around while kissing her forehead.

"Sleep Deprivation, dehydration, starvation, none of my usual non-violent methods even softened her defiance."

Memories of spying on Emily while she babysat her nieces and nephew so Ally and Sarah could attend Feilds ball flashed through Ally's mind, as if called forward by Jackson talking about her. She pushed the, albeit happy, memories of her sister out, refocusing on memories of her daughter and husband. If she let the memories of Emily linger, her anger would win. If her anger won, Jackson won.

"I didn't have a chance to use any of my physical methods on her, but I have a theory that those don't work any better. Not on a Hall at least. My only consolation is that she will be feeling the effects of the psychological torture for quite some time. After all, when I gave her the opportunity to escape, she had a choice to make: escape and save you, or stay and save Kalen. Will that decision haunt her the rest of her life, knowing she didn't *save* either of you?" Jackson asked.

Nothing was working. Ally was already running out of ways to distract her brain from the images Jackson was trying to put in her head. The worst part was she knew he was right. Emily would blame herself for this. She still had her entire life in front of her. The last thing Ally wanted was for Emily to end up petrified and unable to move forward in her life.

"Now, shall we test my theory about the efficacy of using physical torture to get information from a Hall?"

Ally braced herself for what she was certain would come, knowing that she needed to escape. She had a long list of reasons to survive and escape.

Michael

Kate

Lynn

The child she was pregnant with

Cole

And Emily. She needed to make sure Emily didn't blame herself.

TOP SECRET PROMISING GENERATION EYES ONLY

Operation Subversion
Objective: Systematically dismantle the Circle of Fifths

Tuesday

FIELD REPORT:31 October 2000

CLASSIFIED TOP SECRET

06:47 EST McLean Residence; McLean, VA
18:26 EST McLean Residence; McLean, VA

06:47 EST
McLean, Virginia
McLean Residence

I WANTED TO DO SOMETHING. Scratch that; I needed to do something. Since Ally had gone missing, I had a surplus of anxious energy, and no outlet for said energy. Every day I had to sit in class pretending to learn, while the best agents from both the CIA and MI-6 tried to find my sister by chasing the wrong man, I felt my frustration fuel my anger.

I was shocked I hadn't snapped yet.

Sarah, despite being absent most of the time, was still currently my guardian, and as such, she had ordered that I stay in school and let the agents do their job. It was an order I was eager to ignore. Unfortunately, in her absence, Madelyn enforced the tyrannical order. More than once, Madelyn had reminded me I only had a few months of my childhood left, and Sarah was just trying to protect it.

I couldn't wait for my stupid childhood to end. Maybe then Ally wouldn't be the only one who believed in my ability.

Madelyn looked up from the stove as I entered the kitchen. She gave my uniform an appraising look. She turned her eyes back to the stove, but I knew her attention was still focused on me. "The newsletter the school sent out said students could wear a costume today instead of their uniform," Madelyn commented.

"Halls don't celebrate Halloween," I replied.

Madelyn shrugged. "Neither do we. But Neil still took the opportunity to dress up when given the opportunity." She smirked into the eggs she was scrambling. "I also seem to remember you were rather excited to dress up like a ninja on Halloween when you were in kindergarten."

"I'm not a child any more. I didn't feel like dressing up. Can we drop it?" I snapped

Madelyn looked up at me, her eyes feeling like they were piercing through my skin to see what I was hiding underneath.

I squirmed under her gaze, not liking how exposed my thoughts felt. For some reason, as angry and frustrated I was, I didn't want her to know.

After a moment that felt like an eternity, she dropped her eyes as she gave a nod. "William and I discussed something last night, and we want your help with it," she said, stirring the eggs.

"Anything," I replied, trying to hide my desperation. Based on Madelyn's smile, I probably failed, and I wouldn't like what she was about to say.

"We think it would be good for both you and Alyx if you took her trick-or-treating tonight," Madelyn told me.

I should have known it was a trap.

"I'm too old for trick-or-treating," I argued, thinking a logical reply was the best way to get out of it. Trick-or-treating wouldn't help me save my sister, and Madelyn knew that's what my *anything* was for.

Madelyn, however, didn't seem swayed. "Alyx is not. That's why I said you're going to take her."

I shook my head. "Sarah and Neil never let their kids go trick-or-treating."

"Sarah and Neil aren't here—" Madelyn started.

And just like that, I snapped. I didn't even wait to hear her justification before interrupting. "So you will ignore Sarah's rules when it comes to Alyx, *her daughter*, but not for me, her *sister*?"

"Emily…" Madelyn sighed. "I know sitting around while your sister is missing is hard, but William has his best agents—"

"Looking for the wrong person," I interrupted. "But I'm just a child, so what would I know, right?"

Madelyn shook her head. "I never said that, and I know no one else did either."

"You didn't have to. The way everyone is treating me speaks volumes. I mean, Sarah and William didn't even ask to debrief me after I got back. The only questions they asked me revolved around Rafael rescuing me in LA, and they cut me off anytime I tried to report what happened for me to need rescuing to begin with. They've determined they know what happened to Ally, and won't listen to, nevermind consider, my observations, even though it is very likely connected to my mission two weeks ago. But I'm still a minor, so I am only capable of going to school and taking Vee trick-or-treating."

I took a deep breath after finishing my rant. Having said my piece, I finally noticed how tightly Madelyn's lips were pressed together. The closest I'd seen to Madelyn being angry had been the morning after I'd gotten back from LA while Sarah and I were fighting, and it hadn't appeared it took any effort to remain calm as she firmly corrected us.

With my mouth closed, I watched as Madelyn took several deep breaths. I'd done it. I had finally pushed the ever composed Madelyn McLean to the point where she was struggling to keep her composure.

This was one accomplishment I had not been striving to achieve, and did not want to claim proudly.

If I knew what I'd said that had caused it, I would go back in time and prevent myself from saying it. As it was, I wanted to figure out what I'd done so I could take note to never do it again.

"No one debriefed you after LA?" Madelyn finally asked when she'd gotten control.

I shook my head, my voice coming out much softer than before as I answered, "No."

"They know better. I swear, those…" Madelyn seethed under her breath. She must have decided that the eggs were done, because she snapped the stove off, and moved the pan to a burner that hadn't been on.

Watching her putter around the kitchen, it was easy to forget that she was retired CIA. I wasn't sure if anyone had ever told me what she'd done for the CIA, but it seemed like her anger was aimed at her husband and daughter-in-law for not following protocol as it pertained to reporting, not me. I could guess whatever she did, reports were important.

"Have you written your report?" She asked me.

I nodded. "I wrote it the night I got back. But it wasn't an agency mission, so I haven't filed it. Technically, it would probably be classified as a Promising Generation mission, and filing it as such would probably be the best option, especially considering we were going against the Circle of Fifths, and I turned an asset."

Madelyn divided the eggs she'd been scrambling onto two plates, a small plastic one with Winne the Pooh characters for Vee, and a Corelle plate with blue flowers for me. "I will talk to William. He should read your report, but he will likely agree with your assessment. Giving the CIA access to those files would be the same as giving it to the Circle of Fifths."

"That's why I'm so frustrated by Sarah's rule. She treats me like I am incompetent when I'm not," I admitted quietly.

"You are still a minor," Madelyn started. I opened my mouth to protest, but she just stuck a finger up to tell me to wait, and continued. "As a minor, you are required to go to school. *However*, as long as you attend all of your classes, complete and turn in all your homework, and keep up with your studies, I see no reason why you can't continue the mission you started in LA."

I couldn't prevent the smile that snuck onto my face as Madelyn spoke. "Really?" I asked. The offer felt too good to be true.

"This won't get you out of taking Alyx trick-or-treating. Her classmates have been talking about it, and this might be a good first step in helping her relate to her classmates, make some friends, and begin to feel more normal." Madelyn added.

I nodded. I would have paid a far greater price, but I wouldn't let her know that.

"How do I look?" Vee yelled as she ran into the kitchen.

I turned to look at my niece to find her wearing a Space Ranger costume, complete with padded wings. It looked like the costume was meant to be Buzz Lightyear from Toy Story, but Vee was obsessed with the *Adventures of Buzz Lightyear* television series the movie had kicked off, so if I had to guess, she was likely a character from the show.

Vee ran up to me and did a little spin. "Grandma helped me make a Mira Nova costume from the Buzz costume we found."

While Vee stared up at me, waiting for a comment on her costume, I froze. My mind was wandering back to another child staring up at me, and the note for his *Mira Nova.* In all the chaos of leaving LA the way I did, Peter's painting, and the note it held for Vee, had been left behind. I felt a wash of different emotions as my niece's costume reminded me of the painting I should have given her, but overwhelmingly, I felt guilt for forgetting about it.

And confusion. How close were Vee and Peter?

"Do you not like it?" Vee asked, looking herself over when I didn't say anything.

"No, no. I love it. You look very cute," I rushed to reassure her. "I just got lost in thought. You look just like Mira Nova."

Vee beamed up at me. "You mean it?"

"Of course," I told her. I inspected her hair. "Did you color your hair?"

Vee shook her head vehemently. "No. This is my hair."

I looked at Madelyn who smirked at me. How had I not noticed all the red in my niece's hair?

"What's your costume, Emily?" Vee asked me. "Are you a student?"

I turned back to Vee, ready to tell her what I'd told Madelyn about my decision not to dress up, just nicer. However, as my eyes met hers, I could see disappointment.

I wasn't sure why it meant so much to her that I dressed up for Halloween, but she had too many things that made her sad at the moment; I needed to make sure I wasn't one.

"Actually, I'm a spy for Star Command, sent to help you find Zurg's henchmen at school," I replied, coming up with a story about my uniform I hoped would make her happy.

Based on the broad smile on her face, I was guessing I'd succeeded.

"But you can't tell anyone, ok?" I added with a serious face.

"I'm undercover so no one can know." I said, tapping my finger to my lips to indicate it was a secret.

Vee nodded her head, using an invisible key to lock her lips sealed, then handed it to me.

I smiled at the gesture, my heart warming, not only from the fact that she was so willing to keep a secret for me, but that she trusted me with the key of her silence.

Now, I just needed to make sure I deserved it.

18:26 EST
McLean, Virginia
McLean Residence

"GRANDMA, GRANDPA, LOOK HOW MUCH candy I got!"

I hated to admit it, but Madelyn was right when she said trick-or-treating would help Vee. I wasn't sure if it was the fact that she was dressed up as her favorite character from her favorite TV show, or if she was just starting to feel more normal, but she starting to act like the little girl she used to be.

We hadn't been gone for very long—probably no longer than 45 minutes. Madelyn, William, Vee, and I had agreed before we'd left to just stay on the few streets right around us. I hadn't wanted to go too far anyway, especially since Daylight Savings Time had just ended, and even though it was still early, it had already been dark for over an hour.

I locked the door behind myself, slowly following Vee through the house to find her grandparents. I found them in the formal living room. Madelyn and William were sitting next to each other on the couch, and Vee was bouncing up and down in front of them, showing them her full jack-o-lantern bucket.

Madelyn glanced up at me, turned to look at William, then stood up. "Why don't we go find a place to store all this candy?" Madelyn asked Vee, leading her out of the room.

Usually, with Vee in the care of her grandma, I would take full advantage of the break and disappear upstairs to work on my homework. But before I had a chance to even think about it, William made eye contact with me and nodded toward the armchair closest to him on the couch.

I didn't hesitate. I crossed the room and sat down.

"While you and Alyx were gone, Madelyn told me about your conversation this morning," William started.

"I am so sorry. I've just been frustrated, and I snapped this morning…" I apologized. I may not have known why Madelyn scared me, but I wasn't surprised why William did; he wasn't just a parental figure, he was my future boss—as long as I didn't mess up in the next 6 months.

William just shook his head. "I'm not mad. Madelyn was right to correct me, and you have every right to be frustrated. I should have debriefed you when you got back, and I should have asked for your report. Sarah and I let our fear blind us to the fact that you and Ally had been working on something in Los Angeles, and for that, I need to apologize. You have every right to feel frustrated by the way Sarah and I dismissed your attempts to give us a full report. That being said, Madelyn said you wrote a report of your mission; I would like to take action to correct my mistake, and ask for it now."

Even though William had ended with a statement, I knew he was awaiting a reply, so I answered, "I have it upstairs. I can go get it for you." I leaned forward, ready to use my body weight to help me get up.

"Before you go get it, I am going to ask you a question, and I want your unfiltered professional opinion," William said.

I leaned back I to the chair. "Of course," I replied, trying to keep my voice even, despite how nervous it made me to have Deputy Director William McLean ask for my *professional* opinion.

What could I honestly offer him at 17 that he hadn't learned in his decades long career?

"I'm sure reading your report will give me a better picture of the situation, but having been involved in Ally's most recent operation, I want you to tell me who you think has your sister," William said.

"Phil Jackson. From what I have gathered, he is a Circle of Fifths hitter," I answered. "I turned his sister, but he blames Ally for his sister's betrayal."

"When you told Sarah you were caught…" William prodded.

"It was Jackson," I confirmed the question he hadn't asked. "He killed his sister and her husband, incapacitated me, then drove his nephew and I back to LA where I finally escaped."

"What role did Rafael play?" William asked.

I sighed. "I was left alone in the Circle of Fifths substation, so I used the opportunity to escape. As I was running though the parking garage, Rafael showed up. Ally sent him to find me, and gave him instructions for getting me back here."

“So Ally trusts him,” William observed.

I nodded. “Yes.”

William leaned back in his chair, crossing his arms over his chest. “Could Rafael be involved in your sister’s disappearance?”

My heart pounded in my chest. We had officially crossed into an information minefield. I knew I could trust William, but some of the secrets I had weren’t my secrets to share. Still, this was my future; I would have to evaluate the situation and carefully weave my way around the facts I couldn’t share without misconstruing the truth.

As if my hesitance told William everything he needed to know, he leaned back forward. “You’ve been in contact with Rafael since Ally was kidnapped.”

It wasn’t a question; it was a statement. Now I had to figure out how to deny it, because I didn't want to know what the consequences might be for not only disobeying my current guardian, but my future boss.

I must not have come up with an answer fast enough, because William interpreted my silence as guilt.

"I know you don't think he is responsible, and you might be right, but thats not your call to make," William lectured.

Truth it was.

"Rafael is the one who told me Ally was missing," I admitted. "He called me when she missed her check-in."

William stood up and started pacing the living room. “Protocols exist for a reason,” he muttered. “And now, Ally has been missing for days, and we are just finding out we have been looking in the wrong place."

I just stayed quiet, watching William pace back and forth. It had been a while since I'd seen him like this, but I knew he was trying to figure out a solution, and it was better to just fade into the background and let him forget I was the one who told him about the problem.

"You know better, " William finally sighed.

He could have been right, but I had no idea about what.

"I know your parents taught you protocol, and Sarah and Neil have had you practice it, " William added.

"I followed protocol." I argued.

William gave me a look that screamed his disapproval. "You were captured, and we had no idea."

"Ally—"

"Ally was involved in the mission, and clearly also in danger. And don't forget she was in another country, and had to send Rafael to rescue you. Was Rafael in the US?" William interrupted.

"Not that I know…"

William shook his head, "That girl and her secrets could have gotten you killed, " he complained. "They're going to be the death of her," he added, "if she's not dead already."

William's observation hit me like a truck. I didn't want to think about the possibility that Ally could already be dead, but that was the most likely scenario, wasn't it. After all, I had experienced Circle of Fifth's captivity first hand, and I could testify to the fact that they weren't prepared for prisoners.

And I'd seen what happened to their enemies.

Images of my sister laying lifeless like Kyrie suddenly flashed through my mind. Jackson didn't want to just kill Ally, he wanted to make her suffer. At least that much was clear.

Otherwise he would have killed her at the meet.

"If Rafael knew where to find you, does he know where Ally might be?" William asked, drawing me out of my thoughts.

"If he did, I would have already flown to Russia..." I admitted.

"Emily, that is *exactly* what I was talking about," William chastised.

"What do you want me to do when no one takes me seriously?" I asked. I was frustrated by every thing about my situation. It wasn't all William's fault, but he was here.

"Sarah and I ignored your attempts to propose an alternative theory. No matter the outcome, I can tell you we will both be haunted by the what-ifs," William admitted. "But don't let our mistakes justify your carelessness. Don't let our mistakes cause your death too."

I don't know why, but I was surprised by the raw emotion in William's voice. He was Neil's father, not mine. I may have been living with him and Madelyn, and I knew they treated me like family, but I thought that care only went so deep.

Yet William sounded as if he cared about me as if I was his own daughter.

"Why do you care?" I whispered.

Better yet, why do I care that he cares?

Willam watched me carefully before coming over, and extending his hand to me. I placed my hand in his, and he immediately helped me out of the arm chair, then led me to join him on the couch.

He let go of my hand as we both sat down, then asked me a question instead of answering my own.

"Do you know how Sarah and Neil met?"

I tried to think about it, but I couldn't find their meeting in my memories. I could remember Ally meeting Michael vividly, even though I was only 5. I could even remember meeting Addy for the first time, but for the life of me, I couldn't remember meeting Neil. He had just always been there.

I shook my head.

"Before I was promoted and we had to move here to Virginia, we lived in California and our two families were quite close." William began explaining. "We got to watch Sarah and Neil's relationship develop from childhood friends, to a teenaged crush, and eventually dating before it flourished into what it has become."

I wasn't sure why, but hearing how long their relationship had developed made me that much angrier at Sarah for letting it flounder now.

"The point is, Madelyn and I were friends with your parents when they found out they were pregnant with you. Madelyn and I always wanted a big family, but we had a hard time— Neil was our only child, and we accepted that. We are grateful for the blessing he has been in our life. But being friends with your parents ended up being another blessing." William continued.

The way Madelyn doted on Vee had always made sense, but my confusion about how she treated me, and Sarah, and Ally suddenly made more sense.

My mom's family lived in another country, and my dad's older brother, who's name also happened to be William, had moved his family to Pennsylvania and rarely visited. Despite not being old enough to remember it. I could picture William and Madelyn developing a sibling-like relationship with my mom and dad, and becoming an aunt and uncle figure to my siblings.

Me too once I was born.

I wasn't a parent yet, so I didn't have that immense love to compare it to, but I had been surprised by the sometimes overwhelming love I felt for my nieces and nephews.

If that's how William and Madelyn felt about my siblings and I…

"I don't want to stop… I'm a good spy. I don't want to give that up." I admitted.

"I'm not asking you to," William replied. "I'm asking you to be careful. I'm asking you to remember your training, and live by it. But you don't have to figure out what that looks like right now."

"I can be so much more than *just* a student," I insisted. "Besides that, I have a network that gives me intel that can help."

"Do you trust me?" William asked.

I didn't even need to think before I answered, "Yes."

"Then you report directly to me," William said. "Trust me to help you safely act on the intel you receive. "

"Not all of the information I have I can share," I whispered. "I have secrets others have trusted me with."

"That's fine, " William reassured. "Share what you can. Share what is relevant for an action you would like to take. But Emily, what I ask, is that you don't ever think that you are alone. If you need to run, trust me. If you need to hide, trust me. If you need to go undercover, trust me. Let me know, so I can keep you safe, and send aide if you run into trouble."

"I will," I promised.

"Thank you, " William said.

I nodded, looking over at William. "Can I ask for a hug?" I asked.

William smiled. "Of course."

As I wrapped my arms around William, and rested my head on his shoulder like I used to with my dad, I couldn't help but start crying. After my dad died, Sarah and Neil may have taken me in, and provided me with the physical care I needed, but they didn't replace my parents. They didn't try to, and I didn't want them to. Instead, I grew up. I learned how to work through my emotional needs on my own, as I'd watched my adult siblings do.

But at the end of the day, I was still a child. I needed my parents.

I missed my dad.

Even adults needed their parents from time to time. I'd never felt so sure of that fact until this moment. I'd been through hell, and it wasn't even close to being over. But this small moment—this brief conversation with William had given me more comfort than I had been able to find on my own for the past 5 years.

William's fatherly advise felt like, for at least a moment, my father was using William to remind me he would always love me.

William patted my back softly. "Okay. Why don't you bring me your report, and work on your homework. Madelyn can only distract Alyx for so long."

I backed out of the hug, nodded, and wiped the tears from my face.

"You'll be okay," William promised me.

And for the first time in a while, I believed it.

TOP SECRET PROMISING GENERATION EYES ONLY

Operation Subversion
Objective: Systematically dismantle the Circle of Fifths

FIELD REPORT: 2 November 2000

CLASSIFIED TOP SECRET

06:33 EST McLean Residence; McLean, VA
11:30 EST Potomac School; McLean, VA
17:45 EST McLean Residence; McLean, VA

Thursday

06:33 EST
McLean, Virginia
McLean Residence

I RUBBED THE SLEEP FROM my eyes as I opened the door of the bedroom I shared with Vee to trudge down the hall to the bathroom. I had never been a morning person, and the three hour time change I'd experienced moving from California to Virginia hadn't helped. Since I'd gotten back from my failed trip, it had only gotten worse: as I internally complained about how early it was, I was immediately hit by an overwhelming sense of guilt, knowing that I was waking up in my own bed, and Ally was *who-knows* where.

My new guilt-ridden morning ritual was interrupted as I heard William call my name. I turned to see him walking past the partially open door I had just come out of.

"Madelyn is going to get Alyx ready for school this morning," he told me.

I blinked a couple of times while taking a deep breath to try wake up a little bit more.

Probably seeing the confusion on my face, William decided to explain, "I read your report yesterday, and there are some things I want to go over with you. I think you might be able to help us find your sister."

Hearing that he was going to allow me to help find Ally flipped a switch in my brain, and I was suddenly wide awake. "Absolutely. What do you need from me?" I asked.

William shook his head with a small smile. "Get ready for school, then meet me in the office," he told me as he walked away.

Suddenly, I couldn't get ready for school fast enough. After taking care of what I needed to in the bathroom, I rushed back to the bedroom, throwing on the uniform I'd prepared the night before, then tossed my backpack over my shoulder.

By 6:40, I was running down the stairs. As I hit the bottom of the stairs, I turned right, ran through the hallway leading to the kitchen, then navigated around the island to drop my backpack in the mud room between the kitchen and the garage. When I spun around to go to William's office, I came face to face with Madelyn, with arms crossed.

"Good morning Madelyn," I greeted, then tried to move to walk around her.

Madelyn shook her head. "Where do you think you're going?" She asked.

"To talk to William," I replied.

Madelyn raised an eyebrow. "Aren't you forgetting something?"

"He told me you would get Alyx ready for school," I said slowly, thinking that was what she was talking about.

Madelyn turned and pointed to a plate of breakfast on the counter top.

I looked from the plate of breakfast, to the door to Williams office, before looking back at Madelyn.

She rolled her eyes. "You don't have to eat it at the counter. You can take it with you to William's office. He already has his. But you *will* finish it before you and Alyx leave for school. Understood?"

I nodded. "Yes, ma'am."

"Good," Madelyn replied, finally letting a smile crack her steely facade. "Now get going. I don't want you to make Alyx late for school. Remember our agreement. Until you are done with school, your spying is not to interfere with—"

"School," I finished. "I know. Thank you."

Madelyn nodded, letting me past her. I picked up the plate she'd prepared, grabbed the fork she'd set out, and carried it through the family room to the open door of William's office.

William looked up from the papers he was looking over, holding a piece of bacon as he took a bite of it. As he chewed his bite, he pointed to the chair I had occupied just over a week ago. I took a seat, finding a clear section of the desk to place my plate of food. I used the side of the fork to cut through the whites of the fried egg Madelyn had made for me, placing a bite in my mouth.

After he had finished his piece of bacon, William wiped the grease off his hand, before picking up a folder and handing it to me. I finished putting my last bite of egg in my mouth, feeling the warmth of the yoke burst in my mouth as I began chewing and set my fork down. Taking the folder from William, I discovered he was returning the report I'd written.

"I have plenty of questions, especially about my grandson, but the most pressing issue we have at the moment is about the asset you turned," William started.

Chewing as slowly as I could, I used the time it bought me to calm down and focus. Elisabeth. He had questions about Elisabeth.

Once my mouth was empty, I asked, "What about her?"

"Has she proven her loyalty? How do you know she's not the one who betrayed you?" William asked.

He had a fair point, but somehow, I knew she hadn't. He wasn't asking for my gut reaction though. He was asking for observations and facts.

Now I just needed to figure out which of those my subconscious had picked up to tell me she could be trusted. Might as well start at the beginning.

"When I read Cole's report, the way he described Officer Steven's rescue gave me the confidence to approach her. When I did, she was very forthcoming about her involvement in the Circle of Fifths, why she was, and extremely apologetic she couldn't save Annie." I reported.

"How do you know that it wasn't a move made to gain your trust?" William asked.

He was wrong. I knew that. I could feel myself getting frustrated, but how did I know that? "She doesn't want her son trapped in the Circle of Fifths like she is. She gave me a list of all of the Circle of Fifths agents involved in the Promising Generation."

"So she's the one who told you Kyrie McKenzie was also Circle of Fifths, and possibly worth turning?" William clarified.

"Yes," I replied. "She also gently brought up the subject to test the waters before I approached them."

"The Circle of Fifths could have set it up," William commented.

He was playing devil's advocate, I knew that. He was showing me all the alternatives to the way I had interpreted the situation to make sure I was 100% certain of Elisabeth's loyalty. And I was. Despite William pointing out how she could have manipulated me at every turn, I somehow *knew* she hadn't.

Not being able to convince William of that was frustrating.

"She has no reason to be loyal to the Circle of Fifths," I argued. "George Carlyle has used his Circle of Fifths connections to get her transferred away from their son, and instead of asking me to cancel her transfer, she simply asked me to keep him safe, and get George transferred as well. Then she helped me turn the last remaining member of the Circle of Fifths who would be left in the Promising Generation."

William nodded. "But Kyrie's death leaves you with no one, and unless you'd escaped, no one would even know what names Officer Stevens had given you."

"If Elisabeth was loyal and still reporting to the Circle of Fifths, I wouldn't be here right now," I admitted. "Jackson would have known I was the one who had flipped his sister. He would have killed me when he killed Kyrie, not keep me alive to get Ally."

William smiled, then handed me a phone. "Did you set up protocols?"

I took the phone from William slowly, confused by his sudden shift. "You don't actually think she betrayed me?" I asked.

William shook his head. "No. But if you are going to handle assets who are undercover in the Circle of Fifths, I needed to make sure you trusted yourself. I saw her loyalty in your report, but I needed to make sure you recognized it," William told me. "There will be times while handling assets that the line between friend and foe will be difficult to see, and your instinct will be instrumental to your success."

"Not to mention the protocols I failed to set up," I added.

"You would have if things hadn't blown up mere hours after you recruited your assets," William said. "Do you have a way to contact Officer Stevens?"

I shook my head. "I had her phone number, but I had to ditch the phone, and it probably wouldn't be safe anyway. Kyrie contacted me on that number to let me know she'd been burned." I tried to think of alternatives I could use to safely get a message to Elisabeth. For all I knew, she could think I *was* dead. After all, news of Kyrie's death had probably spread like wildfire through Sarah's old team. "Wait, unless she has already been transferred, I know where she will be this afternoon. I could leave a message with her son's teacher to have her call me. With the time difference she should call after I'm done with school."

"What time, specifically?" William asked.

"If Mrs. Jones gives her the message right when she gets there, and she decides to make the call immediately, it could be 12:30 or 1 pm Pacific time, so 3:30 or 4 o'clock. When I approached her there two weeks ago, we left after art time, which is about when I'd expect a call. That was around 2, so 5 our time." I answered.

"Does George know she helps out at Peter's school?" He asked.

"I don't think so," I replied.

William nodded. "It makes sense why she was so particular about her departure time. She is reporting to Langley tomorrow morning, but she insisted she couldn't fly out of LAX until 5 pm tonight."

At least she would have a chance to see Peter one last time. I wondered if she would tell him she was leaving. I glanced at my watch, doing the quick math to figure out what time it was in California.

4 am was a little early to send a teacher an email, in my opinion.

"My computer literacy class is 3rd Period. I can send Mrs. Jones the email then. That would probably be a little better than sending her an email so early," I voiced aloud, making a plan. "I'll tell her that Elisabeth agreed to let me interview her for an assignment I'm doing, but I lost my phone while I was in town, so I lost her number, and ask if she can give my number to Elisabeth so she can give me a call."

"That sounds like a solid plan. I will work from home today, so I can be here when she calls. I would like to assist you in setting up a meet. If she is comfortable, I would like to meet her to let her know you have the support of the CIA," William pointed at the phone he'd given me, adding "Make sure you give her this number. If anyone pulls records on this number, I have it's origins hidden behind shell corporations. If anyone digs deep enough, they'll find it belongs to the department Elisabeth was just transferred to."

I picked up the phone, looking at the small flip phone. "Is it a secured line?"

William nodded.

The phone looked so ordinary. It was surprising that it could be a secure line. Then again, I knew from training that the line could only be as secure as either side of the phone call was. If I made a call in front of enemy operatives, the information shared would be leaked, no matter how secure the phone was.

11:30 EST
McLean, Virginia
Upper School, Potomac School

MY EYES WATCHED THE TEACHER as he stood in front of the computer lab. A projector was displaying his screen as he explained how to use Microsoft Excel, showing us each step he was explaining to us.

This was one of the classes that I *really* didn't need to take, but was required to by the school. I wasn't bored because I didn't see the point of using computers—like some of my classmates. I actually really enjoyed learning about computers and how they could make our lives easier. No, I was bored because this class was teaching the basics, and I had either already learned them from the Promising Generation, and had taught myself more advanced features.

Certain that I wasn't going to miss anything I didn't already know, and that the teacher wasn't paying close enough attention to notice me sending an email, I minimized the window with Excel, and opened Outlook. After quickly glancing up at the teacher, I clicked the button to create a new email and typed in Mrs. Jones' email address from the notes I'd taken this morning when William and I had looked it up, then added the words *Small Favor* in the subject line.

Once I had the email properly addressed, I quickly typed my message.

Hey Mrs. Jones,

I was wondering if you could do me a small favor. When I helped out in your class two weeks ago, I asked Ms. Stephens if she would let me interview her for a homework assignment I have due next week, and she agreed. Unfortunately, I lost my phone before I left town, and now I don't have her number. She told me she typically helps out on Thursdays, so I was hoping you could give her my number (it's changed). It's (202) 254-2401.

Thanks,

Emily Hall

I glanced back up at the teacher, making sure I could still catch up to where he was, then read through my email to make sure I'd spelled everything correctly, and that I had transcribed the number William gave me that morning correctly.

Satisfied, I moved my cursor up to the send button, right as the teacher said "Miss Hall, are you still with us?"

I looked up at the teacher as I hit the button on the mouse to click the button and send the email. "Yes," I replied, and my eyes flicked to the screen to make sure I did in fact know what he had just explained.

The teacher gave me an appraising look, clearly not believing me. He began to walk back towards my computer, so with my eyes still on him, I made sure I knew where my cursor was on the screen, and carefully moved it up to the corner of the window to close Outlook, then brought Excel back up onto my screen. He had spent most of the class so far teaching us how to create formulas, and he had us using the *Sum* formula over and over again, probably hoping the repetition would help us learn it.

I was behind at least 3 formulas.

Fortunately, since I was more familiar with Excel than most of the class, I knew a shortcut, and I quickly dragged the formula over to copy it into the three boxes I was behind.

Unfortunately, I hadn't been planning on getting caught, so when the teacher got to my computer, not only did it look like I'd had no problem keeping up with his demonstration, but he could also see I knew Excel much better than I had let on so far. In my boredom yesterday, I had used the conditional formatting feature to highlight the boxes red, yellow, or green depending on the totals. His demonstration hadn't gotten to that feature yet, so it was supposed to be a very bland black and white, and mine was definitely very colorful.

"You've used Excel before," he said.

I swallowed. "A little," I admitted. "I like computers though, and I sometimes play around with it a little to figure out other features."

"Please stay focused on what I am showing you," he admonished, walking back up to the front of the class.

I quietly blew out my breath. If I got bored again, I doubted I could keep myself from playing around any more in Excel, but at least today, I had gotten away with sending my email.

Now all that I had to do was wait.

17:45 EST
McLean, Virginia
McLean Residence

THE CALCULUS BOOK IN FRONT of me was doing little to distract me from the ticking clock on the office wall. William was working—at least he was doing a better job of pretending to work than I was.

Madelyn walked into the office, throwing a dish towel over her shoulder. She caught me looking at the clock yet again, instead of solving the problem I had been trying to solve for the last twenty minutes.

"Up, both of you," Madelyn ordered. "You have been waiting for this phone call since Emily got home from school, and it's time to eat dinner. Bring the phone if you must, but I can't let you two neglect yourselves while you wait for a call that may or may not come."

"She'll call any minute," I argued. "She *will* call. I know she will."

"*If* she calls in the next half hour while we're eating dinner, you and William can leave to answer it," Madelyn replied.

"But—" I started to argue some more.

"Come on Emily," William said, getting up from his chair. "We're just waiting right now anyway way. We might as well eat while we wait."

I begrudgingly got up, following Madelyn and William out of the office. Walking out felt a lot like giving up, and even if I knew it wasn't true, I hated the feeling, so I took my time.

William and Madelyn were to the kitchen by the time I was halfway through the family room. William walked behind Vee, who was already seated at the table, patiently waiting for the rest of us. He stopped, placing his hand on her little head, then rubbed it, messing up her hair.

"Hey!" She said. She gave William a chastising look she had learned from Sarah. On an adult, the look worked, but on Vee, it just looked comical.

"How is my little star today?" William asked, tickling her sides.

Vee fought the laugh. She tried as hard as she could to remain serious, but failed, her giggles filling the room.

I lifted my foot to cross the threshold between the family room and kitchen when I heard the electronic beeps of the Nokia ringtone coming from the phone in my hand. I looked down at the tiny digital screen, seeing the 909 area code I had come to know well from living in Southern California.

My eyes went from the phone to William as it began to repeat the tune.

"No phones at dinner," Vee said, reminding me of the rules.

As she did, William said, "Answer it."

So I did just as William had coached me hours earlier, flipping open the phone, holding it up to my ear, and demanding, "Identify," to answer the phone.

"M 2511 ES," the person on the other end replied. "Challenge," she added.

I nodded at William. This was Elisabeth. She hadn't identified herself the way William had told me a CIA officer would. But technically, I wasn't a CIA handler. I wasn't old enough to even join the CIA, so despite calling a CIA number, she identified herself in a way very few people would understand. If it was a trap, she could still maintain her cover.

I turned to walk back to William's office. "Camellia. Gold. 2401." I answered her challenge the same way I'd answered her son's a couple weeks ago.

"Thank heavens," Elisabeth replied. "I heard about Kyrie, and then I didn't hear anything from you. I was scared they'd gotten you too."

"I'm alive. And safe," I said.

William walked past me, sitting back down behind his desk. He gestured for me to put the phone on speaker, so I did.

"Listen, Elisabeth. We need to meet and discuss protocols," I told her. "I also have some questions I'm hoping you can answer."

Elisabeth sighed through the phone. "I'm at the airport. I'm getting ready to fly—"

"To Virginia, I know. You've been transferred," I interrupted. "I'll be in Virginia this weekend."

"How do you know I'm heading back to Virginia?"

I glanced up at William. It wasn't our plan to hide his involvement from Elisabeth. I just had to be very careful about the way I told her. "I still have a couple of friends in the CIA," I replied.

"How do you know they can be trusted?" Elisabeth asked. "Especially with everything you've just found out."

"Because I grew up with Deputy Director McLean," I replied. "And his motivation is just as strong as yours and mine, if not stronger."

"Deputy Director McLean?"

I could hear the disbelief in Elisabeth's voice.

"How can *you* have Deputy Director McLean as a friend in the CIA? And I don't mean that as any disrespect. It's just, you're not even old enough to…"

"I know," I said. "But like I said, he's a close family friend." I glanced at William who raised an eyebrow as if to ask if that's all I thought he was. "He's also my brother-in-law's father, so I guess that makes him family," I added.

William smiled, clearly pleased by me recognizing him as family.

"The point is, his grandson is the one who pointed me to you, and he is my best resource for keeping the promises Ally and I made you." I looked at William who nodded, so I continued. "While I'm in Virginia, William would like to meet you, make good on what we promised for your help, and help me set up the protocols we need to ensure your safety."

"That explains the number," Elisabeth sighed. "I trust you, so if you trust him, I trust him," Elisabeth said. "When and where?"

"Tomorrow. 5 pm. The Potomac School in McLean, Virginia," I answered.

William's eyes went wide, giving me a subtle head shake to say he disagreed with my meeting place.

"The school is having a Fall Festival as a fundraiser. I'll meet you at the caramel apple booth," I finished.

Through the phone, I could hear a woman announce "Now boarding…" over the PA system.

"I'll meet you then," Elisabeth replied, hanging up.

I picked up the phone, snapping it shut before I looked up at William, who did not look happy with me.

"The sooner I meet with Elisabeth, the sooner we can ask her if she has any information that will help us find Ally. But Madelyn said it can't interfere with school, and my English teacher is making my class run the Caramel Apple Booth at the fair tomorrow. If I miss my shift, my grade will be affected. It *is* a public event, though, so two birds, one stone." I explain.

"And if she's followed. If the Circle of Fifths finds Alyx…" William warned.

"They won't," I replied. I stood up, finally ready to join Madelyn and Vee for dinner.

TOP SECRET PROMISING GENERATION EYES ONLY

Operation Subversion
Objective: Systematically dismantle the Circle of Fifths

FIELD REPORT: 3 November 2000

CLASSIFIED TOP SECRET

16:55 EST Potomac School Fall Festival; McLean, VA

16:55 EST
McLean, Virginia
Potomac School Fall Festival

"HOW MUCH IS THIS ONE?" The woman standing at the front of the line for the Caramel Apple booth asked, pointing to one of the apples.

"They're all four tickets," I replied.

The woman counted out some tickets from the envelope she'd been given by the ticketing booth at the entrance, handing them to me. I double checked that there were indeed four of them (or about a dollar's worth), and placed them in the repurposed coffee can my English class had decorated to serve as our cash box for the booth. Her payment received, I handed her the apple she'd pointed out.

"Enjoy," I told her as the apple changed hands.

As she gave me a small smile and walked away, letting the next person in line approach, I glanced over to where William had posted himself, able to both watch me, and the entrance, so he could warn me when he saw Elisabeth show up. From just a quick glance, I knew Elisabeth hadn't entered the festival yet, and returned my attention to the new customer in front of me.

As I handed the next gentleman his apple, the classmate who was replacing me joined me at the booth, helping the last customer in line from our little rush. With all the customers helped, and nothing else to do, I looked at William again. As if I'd timed it perfectly, I watched as William took off his Irish flat hat: our signal for Elisabeth's arrival.

Our last customer walked away, allowing me to turn to my classmate. "I'm off," I told her. I handed her four tickets, choosing an apple from the table. "It has been so hard to look at these for the past hour and not eat one," I admitted, then walked off to the side so it didn't look like I was working the booth any more.

I scanned the crowd walking into the festival, trying to find Elisabeth. If I hadn't already known how talented a spy Elisabeth was, I would have been impressed with her ability to blend in. Until she walked up to the Caramel Apple booth, and I heard her voice asking my classmate for an apple, I couldn't find her.

Somehow, even without a child, she looked like she belonged at this school activity.

"They just look too good to resist," I commented, drawing her attention to me.

She raised the apple up in the air as she walked away from the booth. "I'm supposed to be on a diet, but it's just an apple right?"

"Absolutely," I replied with a smile. Once she was close enough I could drop my voice and she could still hear me, I asked, "How are you doing?"

Elisabeth gave a short head shake. "He still doesn't know," she admitted. "He tried to call me after school, and I couldn't answer because the terms of George's custody agreement explicitly forbid contact."

She took a deep breath. I didn't know what to say to her admission. I wasn't a mother, so I couldn't even begin to imagine the pain she was feeling. "I'm sorry," I softly whispered.

"It's not your fault, and you have nothing to apologize for," Elisabeth said. "I will never regret having Peter. He is the greatest blessing in my life. But getting involved with George and the Circle of Fifths was the greatest mistake of my life. All I can do now is take steps to ensure my mistake doesn't take Peter's life from him, and hope for the best."

I glanced at William who had been helping us with counter surveillance. He was walking towards us with his flat cap placed back on his head, indicating that Elisabeth was clean, and she hadn't been followed.

"William can help us with that," I started.

Elisabeth nodded. "And I'm grateful," as William approached, she nodded to him. "I mean no disrespect by asking this, but why the change of plans?"

I glanced at William. The urgency of us meeting with Elisabeth was because we wanted to ask her for any intel that might help us find Ally, so we had to tell her at some point in this conversation. But if we told her now about Ally being kidnapped, we might scare her off. Kyrie, me, *and* Ally all being targeted by the Circle of Fifths wasn't necessarily something that inspired confidence. On the flip side, not telling her now when she asked, and waiting until we had her commitments would cause her to lose trust in me.

William gave a small nod, answering my unasked question.

"That's one of the things we wanted to talk to you about," I started, but I had no idea how to continue.

As I thought about how to tell Elisabeth that my sister had been kidnapped, she waited patiently in silence. I wish she wouldn't. I wish she would ask questions. I wish she would give me a better opening to start. I wish William could just tell her.

"Ally has been missing since October 24th," I finally said.

"Missing as in she went into hiding, or…"

I sighed. I wish Ally was just in hiding. "No. She was kidnapped. She was last seen in Russia, and she was there to meet with Phil Jackson."

Elisabeth's eyes went wide. "Phil Jackson, as in Phillip Jackson, Kyrie's older brother?"

"I guess. Kyrie just called him Phil," I replied. "I take it you know him."

Elisabeth nodded. "I've met him a couple of times. George idolizes him, so without even knowing his reputation, I'd know Ally meeting with him would be a bad idea. What on earth inspired her to meet with him?"

"How much do you know about what happened to Kyrie?"

"Only what was reported on the news, so not much," Elisabeth replied. "Why? What do you know?"

I sighed. "I was there when Jackson killed her, and he didn't find us in California."

Elisabeth gasped, "How did you get away?"

"I didn't. Not at the safehouse, at least," I admitted. "I was trying to get Kalen out, but when he heard…"

I couldn't finish that statement. How could I have failed him? I was supposed to protect them, and not only did I fail to keep his parents alive, but I let him run straight into his uncle's arms.

William placed a hand on my shoulder, causing me to take a deep breath and focus on the present, and what I needed to do.

"He got the drop on me. When he found out I was Ally's sister, he decided to use me to lure her out. I escaped, but… I can only guess what she was thinking meeting with him, but now she's missing, and I would bet everything I own Jackson has her." I finished.

"If you're right, the chances that we'll find her alive…" Elisabeth sighed.

I nodded. "We have to try. I know you agreed to help us, but I also acknowledge that this is more dangerous than what you signed up for. If you want to back out, I won't blame you. I have already talked to William about what you asked for, and he agreed to transfer George, so you don't have to worry about Peter—"

"Nonsense," Elisabeth interrupted. "I don't care about how dangerous it is. The Circle of Fifths doesn't care about how many people they hurt or kill. They need to be stopped, and if I can help with that, I will. This is the least I can do."

"We can't make any promises that you'll get Peter back," William spoke up for the first time, making it clear that George's transfer wouldn't guarantee she could get visitation. "All I can do is transfer George here to DC so you can keep an eye on Peter."

Elisabeth shook her head. "I don't care. Suddenly fighting George for custody after he was unexpectedly transferred would be a red flag, and as much as I would love to be in Peter's life, it's safer for both of us if I'm not. At least not for the time being."

Elisabeth took a shaky deep breath, clearly trying not to cry. I couldn't imagine being able to make that kind of sacrifice for her son. If I had to choose between never seeing Vee again, or her safety… I don't know that I could do it. I would try to find another option. There was always a third option.

Or maybe my default stage of grief was bargaining. There was always a way out.

"What if George didn't have custody either?" I asked, my brain already cutting a third path through the metaphorical forest.

Elisabeth and William gave me a look that said they weren't sure how what I was suggesting was possible.

"Hear me out," I started. "It might take a little manipulation, but what if we convince George to transfer to DC, but leave Peter in California with the Promising Generation. Jackson already has Kalen, and we know that boy will be brainwashed and conditioned to be a perfect soldier for the Circle of Fifths. If there's a chance we can prevent George from doing the same to Peter, we have to try."

I couldn't let another innocent child, especially one as kind-hearted as Peter, become a soulless killer for a terrorist organization.

"That is going to be quite the manipulation," Elisabeth commented. "George would have to believe it was his idea."

I smirked. I already had an idea of how I might be able to trick him into doing as I wanted him to, but that was an issue for another day. "That's a problem for future me. As long as you don't object to Peter remaining with the Promising Generation, I can do my best to make it happen."

Elisabeth nodded. "If you can get Peter away from his father, I would be forever grateful. No amount of intel I could provide would ever repay you."

"You saved Cole," I replied. "Someone needs to repay you. I think a life for a life is a good start."

Elisabeth took a deep breath. "I suppose that's fair. As for Ally, there's not much I can share, but hopefully it helps," she said, pausing for a moment. "If she went missing in Russia, chances are Jackson was working with a local asset. I don't know very much about the man, but I know he provides most of the cover identities for European operatives. I would start with him."

"Rafael Feilds," I said. "He was involved in setting up the meeting, but he wasn't in the country at the time." I glanced at William, trying not to let my despair overwhelm me.

Jackson had planned this perfectly. *Everyone* was blaming Rafael, but I knew, just *knew* he wasn't involved. I mean, he called to report Ally missing. If he was honestly responsible for Ally being missing, he was a much better operative than anyone had given him credit for. But more than that, if we found out he was in fact more involved than he had already admitted to me, my trust in my own judgement would be shot.

Elisabeth took my moment of silence to evaluate me carefully. "You're better than I gave you credit for," she commented. "I didn't even know his name."

"Considering his familial connection, and where Ally was when she disappeared, Rafael has been the focus of the CIA and MI:6 investigation," William explained. "We blindly believed he was the person who had Ally, despite evidence to the contrary. It wasn't until Emily corrected me, and gave me a report of what happened in LA that I even considered someone else could be involved."

Elisabeth continued to regard me, a look of admiration and respect in her eyes. It felt a little uncomfortable. She had said I was better than she gave me credit for, but it wasn't my talent that had led me to the intel I knew. Ally had trusted me with her secrets, meaning I knew far more than I cared to.

"Do you know where Jackson might take Ally?" I asked. "I mean, he took me to the Circle of Fifths base in LA, but it's clear that those aren't exactly equipped for prisoners."

"You really don't know anything about Phillip Jackson, do

you?" Elisabeth sighed. "Jackson is an interrogator, and a good one at that. He is stationed in the Middle East, and works primarily at CIA black sites."

I closed my eyes and took some deep breaths. After seeing what he'd done to his sister, I already had an idea of what Ally was going through, but to hear Elisabeth actually tell me what Jackson's job was… I couldn't let myself imagine what Ally was going through because I might not be able to continue to function and do what needed to be done to find my sister and bring her home.

"And he probably has a few of his own," I added, eyes closed. "So she probably isn't in Russia anymore, and could be anywhere in the world."

Elisabeth shook her head. "I wouldn't be so sure. You have personally experienced Jackson's habits."

"He drove me a few hours back to LA," I answered.

"You, maybe. But that's because he had other things to take care of, but it sounds like he followed his usual modus operandi for his sister."

I nodded, remembering what Kylie had said her brother's MO was. "Cut the power and communication lines, then waited just long enough to give the illusion of hope before breaching."

"And keeping his target at location," Elisabeth added. "Jackson prefers to finish his job in his targets' home, because it adds a psychological element."

I took a deep breath. "Ok, he's a sadist." It would have been a lie to say I wasn't rattled. You heard stories about men like that on the news, but the fact that I'd met him... I'd *survived* him.

And now Ally was with him.

"But he met Ally at a cafe, and she doesn't live in Russia," I said.

"Was she staying somewhere in Russia?" Elisabeth asked.

I shook my head. "No. It was meant to be a quick trip in and out."

"Ok," Elisabeth exhaled. "Transporting a prisoner involves a lot of risks, and those risks increase the farther you take them. Since Jackson doesn't usually transport his targets, we'd have to assume that he stayed in Russia. I know when he's needed to, he's used an empty CIA safehouse. He probably would have taken her to one that was close, but secluded enough to be left alone."

I looked at William, hoping he would know of one that fit that description.

When he made eye contact with me he gently shook his head.

"I don't have CIA safehouses memorized. I'd have to look into it," he said. He turned to look at Elisabeth. "But that information is *extremely* useful."

I tried to not be disappointed. I knew that we now had *much* more information than we'd had before this meeting, but it would take a couple days for William to look into it, then probably a couple more to put together a team to rescue Ally. Talking in *days* when a life was hanging in the balance, and every *second* counted was painful.

"Let's discuss protocols," William said, redirecting this conversation to its main purpose.

At least I had something else to focus on while I waited.

TOP SECRET PROMISING GENERATION EYES ONLY

Operation Subversion
Objective: Systematically dismantle the Circle of Fifths

FIELD REPORT:5 November 2000

CLASSIFIED TOP SECRET

18:16 MSK Unlisted Black site; Moscow, Russia
10:25 EST McLean Residence; McLean, VA
14:35 UTC Incident Report
14:56 EST McLean Residence; McLean, VA

18:16 MSK
Moscow, Russia
Unlisted Blacksite

"I'M GOING TO ASK THIS again," Jackson seethed. "How did you find our LA safehouse?"

"Go to hell," Ally breathed between attempts to catch her breath.

Jackson leaned in close enough Ally could smell his breath, and feel the displaced air of his words as he told her, "If you don't answer my question, you'll never get the chance to send me there."

Ally's breath rattled as she shot Jackson a glare. That small effort was almost more than she could bear. After all, the venom Jackson had given her was making her nauseous, and her vision was blurry.

"Your niece didn't just stumble across a Circle of Fifths safehouse, just like you didn't just show up at my sister's house. Alyxandrie knew it was a Circle of Fifth safehouse, just like you knew my sister was Circle of Fifths. The question is how."

On the plus side, the symptoms of the venom, which Ally knew were supposed to encourage her to talk, gave her something to focus on while ignoring Jackson's questions.

"The girl must have seen a photo of the safehouse," Jackson

continued. "I just want you to tell me if my sister was the only traitor, or if she was working with someone else."

Ally laughed at Jackson's question, which devolved into coughs. *Maybe Alyx is smarter than you give her credit for*, she thought. No one knew how close the Circle of Fifths was until she found them.

"Sir," one of Jackson's guards said before he had a chance to ask his question again. "It's time to give her the anti-venom."

"That's fine," Jackson replied, backing away from her. "She's given me all she will for the night."

If she wasn't still trying to catch her breath, Ally would have laughed at Jackson again. She hadn't given him anything, and she never would.

Jackson watched as his guard approached Ally, using a needle to give her the anti-venom for whichever venom he had decided to use this time. She had lost count of how many venoms Jackson had used on her. At this point, they all made her feel miserable, and the anti-venom didn't help her feel much better. It was too late. The damage was done. Her body was shutting down.

As the needle slipped out of her skin, black dots started to appear in her vision. She was exhausted, partially because she wasn't sure when the last time was that she actually slept, not just passed out.

She was also so tired of fighting to stay alive.

What was she fighting for anyway?

Ally closed her eyes, letting the darkness sweep her away as Jackson gave orders to look into Alyxandrie McLean.

10:25 EST
McLean, Virginia
McLean Residence

WE WERE ON OUR WAY out the door to church when William's cell phone rang.

"McLean," he answered, then listened quietly while someone on the other end talked.

Madelyn ushered Vee out the door to help her get in the car, but I stood frozen, watching him closely as he received the brief 15 second report.

William's poker face was better than I had given him credit for, because by the time he answered, "Thank you," and hung up the phone, I still had no idea whether or not the call had been about Ally.

Or if it had been good or bad news.

"Madelyn, would you mind taking the girls to church by yourself? I'm going to have to head into the office," William hollered to his wife as he stuck his phone back in his pocket.

Madelyn simply nodded, closing the car door having gotten Vee in her booster seat. She walked over to William, and took the car keys from him.

"Come on, Emily," she said, walking back to the car.

Based on Madelyn's reaction, I could guess that this happened all the time, so I still didn't have enough information to guess whether or not William's call had anything to do with his search for safehouses in Russia.

I guess it was time to just ask.

"Was that about Ally?"

Madelyn turned around at my question, while William seemed to not even react.

"He couldn't tell us even if it was," Madelyn told me. "Come on, let's go to church."

"You can't send a CIA team for her. There are too many Circle of Fifths members in the CIA for any operation you put together to stay covert. Before you have a chance to even touch Russian soil, Jackson will have killed her." I reasoned.

"If you don't leave soon, you'll be late," William said instead of answering me.

I wanted to scream. There was no way I could just go to church if there was a possibility William knew Ally's location.

"You promised as long as it doesn't affect my school performance, I could help find Ally," I reminded him.

He said nothing.

"Please, I can help," I pleaded.

William shook his head. "Go to church. I'll call you if you can help."

I stared at William for another moment, all the ways I could help flashing through my mind. At the same time, I knew that without being in Russia, I could really only help in an advisory capacity, and I was sure William was just as capable at coming up with ideas as I was.

I'd figure out how to get myself to Russia, but I couldn't with out breaking my promise to not let it interfere with school. While I knew finding Ally would be worth almost any consequence they could impose, I knew ditching school and running off to Russia would be forfeiting *all* privileges to participate in anything tangentially related to espionage, including running Elisabeth as an asset.

I was also hoping to convince Sarah or William to give me control of the Promising Generation. If I had control, there was so much I could do to help those kids, and probably even catch the Circle of Fifths.

If I did what I wanted right this moment, I'd lose a chance at dismantling the Circle of Fifths in the future.

As much as I hated it, and as difficult as it was, I nodded at William, letting him know I understood, then I turned and joined Madelyn in the car, claiming the front passenger seat since William wasn't coming.

Then I started praying.

US TOP SECRET PROMISING GENERATION EYES ONLY

INCIDENT REPORT: 5 November 2000
CLASSIFIED TOP SECRET

[TS//PG] 1435 UTC. After receiving intelligence regarding unauthorized use of an agency safehouse in Moscow, Redorca enlisted the help of a trusted acquaintance in Russia and gave her enough information to decide whether she should act herself, or contact local authorities.

Then he waited for a call.

14:56 EST
McLean, Virginia
McLean Residence

THE THREE HOURS OF CHURCH had never felt so long in my entire life. It had been nearly impossible to focus on the talks and lessons. Usually when my mind wandered a bit, it wasn't terribly difficult to catch myself and find a way to reengage, but not today. Today, all I could think of was what William had come up with to rescue Ally from the safehouse, and whether or not she would be alive.

It was agonizing.

After I had *finally* made it through the third hour, I had been the first one out of my class, and had quickly picked Vee up from hers, only to be stuck waiting almost half an hour for Madelyn, who had been chatting with *anyone* she saw.

Now that we were finally pulling up in front of the house, it had been over four hours since William had received the call that may or may not have been about Ally.

If I'd been in the right mindset, I'd have been able to consider the fact that William not calling me could be a positive. He hadn't needed my help, which made sense. But he also hadn't called to tell us that they'd found Ally.

What if she wasn't there? What if she was dead?

My stomach sank as Madelyn backed into the driveway, and a black SUV with government plates pulled up in front of the house. The FBI loved to use SUVs *exactly* like that one, and the only reason someone from the FBI would be here…

I didn't even need to complete my thought as I watched Neil get out of the SUV with a bag over his shoulder and run up to the front door.

If Neil was home, we weren't walking into the house to be greeted with good news.

The moment the car was parked, I was out of the car and halfway to the door. I charged right into the house, following Neil's discarded bag to find him with a distraught Sarah wrapped in his arms. I tore my eyes away from my sister and her husband to find William.

"You found her," I croaked.

William just gave a subtle nod.

"How bad was the body?" I asked, even though I wasn't sure I wanted to know.

William shook his head. "She's alive. She's in bad shape, covered in bruises and in and out of consciousness, but alive. Walked herself right up to the UK Embassy, and told them who she was before passing out."

For the first time since Rafael called me twelve days ago, I was able to take a full, deep, unhindered breath of relief.

"She's going to be okay," I whispered.

But if that was the case, why was Neil here, and why wasn't Sarah relieved.

There was bad news I hadn't heard yet.

"But?" I asked William.

William sighed. "She is currently on a helicopter being flown to the Feild's choice of hospital so she can be evaluated, but the medic at the embassy didn't think it looked good. She definitely lost the baby."

The baby? Ally was pregnant?

I would have loved to ask why I wasn't told, or why she had decided to meet with Jackson knowing the risks, but I knew Ally was the only one who could answer those questions.

Instead I asked, "How far along?"

"Doctor said about 3 months," William answered.

At least it sounded like William hadn't been told either, so it wasn't just me who didn't know.

"Thirteen weeks," Sarah mumbled as she turned her head out of Neil's shoulder. Whether Neil wouldn't let her go, or she didn't want out of the hug, I didn't know, but it was nice to see them rebuilding their relationship.

We all went silent for a moment, unsure what to say. No words would make us feel better.

The silence was broken as Vee squealed, "Mommy! Daddy!" as she ran over to join their hug.

Neil finally released Sarah from his hug to smile at his little girl who had an arm wrapped around both his and Sarah's legs. He bent down, picking Vee up so she was face-to-face with him. "How has my little star been?" He asked her.

"Good!" she replied. "I started school, and I made friends and, and I got to go trick-or-treating with Emily, and I learned how to write my name, and grandma Madi is teaching me how to read, and, and…and I missed you."

Neil laughed. "I missed you too, Alyx," he admitted, then gave her a kiss on her forehead.

Vee spun her head to look at her mom, then frowned. "Mommy, why are you sad?"

Sarah shook her head, wiping away her tears as she gave Vee a sad smile. "Just got some bad news about my sister."

"Like I'm sad about Cole and Annie?" Vee asked.

Sarah nodded her head, more tears escaping as I felt my eyes and throat begin to burn as I fought my own.

Vee reached out from Neil's arms to wrap her arms around her mom's neck. "It's ok mom," she said, her voice all serious. "I can help you on your sad days, just like Emily has helped me on mine."

And just like that, I lost the battle against my tears.

Neil moved back in so he could join Vee in hugging Sarah and providing her comfort.

My sister had no idea how lucky she was.

"When do we leave?" Madelyn asked.

"As soon as we're packed," William replied. "Michael sent his jet for us."

"Are we going on a trip?" Vee asked.

"We are," Neil told her. "We're going to London."

"I *love* London!" She exclaimed. "Ally promised to take me exploring."

Sarah used her finger to brush an unruly curl out of her daughter's face. "Ally can't take you, but can I take you instead?"

"Sure mom," Vee replied. "I can show you all the secret rooms Ally showed me last time."

"I'd love that," Sarah said, and I could tell she meant it. "Would you come pack with me?"

"Yes," Vee answered. "Can daddy come with us?"

"I'd love to," Neil told her, handing Vee off to Sarah.

I watched as what was left of my sister's family left the room, Sarah carrying Vee, with Neil just behind them, a hand gently resting on the small of Sarah's back, probably meant to comfort and remind her she wasn't alone.

Once they had left the room, and were far enough away to be out of earshot, William looked at me.

"We found her alive because of you," he told me. "If you hadn't insisted I explore other options, I never would have checked Agency safehouses, and she wouldn't be on her way home right now."

"But you said it doesn't look good," I whispered.

"You have given your family a great gift," William said. "In our line of work, we rarely get the chance to say goodbye. But your insistence has given us that. Not to mention Ally gets a chance at survival. Even if she doesn't, you gave her a chance she didn't have with Jackson. You saved her from who knows how much more agony, before dying alone."

Well when said like that.

"Why don't you go pack," William suggested.

I just nodded, heading upstairs. I needed a distraction to prevent a breakdown.

TOP SECRET PROMISING GENERATION EYES ONLY

Operation Subversion
Objective: Systematically dismantle the Circle of Fifths

FIELD REPORT:10 November 2000

CLASSIFIED TOP SECRET

14:24 GMT St. Thomas Hospital; London, UK

14:24 GMT
London, UK
St. Thomas Hospital

WHEN WE'D ARRIVED IN LONDON, the doctors had already run a full battery of test, and the news they'd given us was anything but good. Based on the anti-venoms they found in her blood, they guessed her organ damage had been caused by rattle snake and synanceia venoms, but they'd been confused how she'd ended up with those venoms in her system, because they hadn't found any stings or bites, and she hadn't been found someplace she'd naturally encounter *one* of those animals, never mind both of them.

Knowing who had had her, I unfortunately knew *exactly* how she'd ended up like this. Clearly, Jackson thought she had some information he wanted, and had used some creative methods to try and get that information.

It was hard not to let my mind wander to the dark places I could imagine Ally had been in while she was missing. She was rarely conscious, so my shifts keeping her company were slow and boring. I had already completed all of my homework for the day, so I was counting ceiling tiles, trying to keep my mind off of the hell my sister had been through.

"Emily?"

I startled, hearing my name when I didn't expect to. I was facing the door, so I knew it wasn't one of Ally's nurses, nor another family member popping in for a visit; I would have seen them come in the door.

There was one possibility for who could be talking to me, but I didn't want to look and be disappointed when I realized I had imagined it.

Braced and ready to see no change like any of my other shifts, I turned to look at Ally. Instead of seeing the scene I was prepared for—Ally unconscious with her oxygen tube under her nose—I was greeted by Ally's familiar blue eyes.

"You're awake!" I exclaimed, surprised.

Ally laughed, but ended up coughing, so I grabbed her glass of water, holding it for her so she could sip some through the straw.

Once she had stopped coughing, and I helped her settle back in the hospital bed, I got up.

"Where are you going?" Ally asked.

"I need to let someone know you are awake," I answered. "I'm sure Michael would love to talk to you."

"I talked to Michael last night, and I'm sure I'll talk to him again tonight," Ally told me. "I've already talked to mom, Sarah, and Dylan as well. You're the only one who hasn't been here when I was awake."

I couldn't help but stare at Ally. We had set up a rotation, making sure someone was always with Ally. We'd all promised we would let each other know if Ally woke up so we got a chance to say goodbye. I had ended up with the longest shift during the day between lunch and dinner, which I guessed was because they were excluding me from the investigation—again. Michael spent his nights here so he could spend his days with Kate; he was the only one we hadn't asked to call us if she woke up.

"We promised we'd call…" I started, torn between wanting to keep my promise and being upset no one else had.

"I asked them not to," Ally admitted. "I wanted to talk to each of you one at a time first. You can call next time, I promise."

"Ally," I sighed. "You can tell me when you go home."

Ally shook her head. "You and I both know I'm not surviving."

"Don't say that," I complained.

"The only reason I survived as long as I did was because I couldn't die without saying goodbye, and I needed to make sure you didn't blame yourself," Ally admitted.

"Ally…" I trailed off, not knowing what to say. What could I say to that?

"My choices got me here, not yours, and I need you to remember that," Ally continued.

"I got caught," I whispered. "If I hadn't gotten caught…"

"Jackson still would have come after me, and you wouldn't have been available to help William find me," Ally interrupted.

"You still would have been protecting Kyrie's family, and no one would have known to look for Jackson."

"Don't try to spin me getting caught as a good thing," I said.

Ally shook her head. "I'm not saying it was. My point is that Jackson would have come for me either way. I am not paying for your mistakes."

"Ok, you have absolved me of my guilt, can I call our siblings now?" I asked. I didn't want to have this conversation, so if I could avoid it…

"Not yet," Ally told me. "When I'm gone, I need you to do something for me."

"Maybe my avoidance wasn't clear enough—"

"You need to go to college, and do anything but join the family business," Ally said.

I froze. I must have heard her wrong. There was no way *Ally* of all people was telling me I couldn't be a spy.

"I know I messed up with Kyrie's family, and I've lost Kalen because of it, but I've learned from my mistakes. William has helped me set up protocols for Elisabeth, and—"

"There are two people Jackson will want to come after once I'm dead: you and Alyx. Rafael has already helped me with Alyx—"

It was my turn to interrupt Ally. "What are you talking about?"

Ally let out a mournful sigh. "The entire time Jackson had me, he asked me different variations of the same question—how did Sarah's kids find the safehouse."

"Someone gave him access to the interview Vee did with the police," I said.

Ally swore, like a real, American swear word. Not a French expression of displeasure. Not a French swear word. Not one of the English expressions she'd picked up from her husband.

That's how I knew things were *really* bad. I'd never heard her swear before, and I'd given her plenty of reasons to swear over the years.

"What's wrong?" I asked her.

Ally shook her head. "Alyx is just in more trouble than I thought. I don't think I said anything that would especially endanger her, but..."

"What *exactly* was Jackson asking you?" I asked.

"If we had more than just his sister as a mole. He was convinced Alyx saw or overheard something that led her to attack their safehouse," Ally reported.

"Ok," I said. I could see why Ally was concerned. A five-year-old had found their safehouse, and had cost them years of research, and more than a couple agents.

They had already tried to kill her, both in the house, and since. Now it seemed, they had sent their best interrogator after her.

"How is Rafael helping with Vee?" I asked.

"He has agreed to take credit for my death," Ally replied.

As if I hadn't just had to fight William to convince him otherwise.

"What on earth does that do to help?" I asked, the frustration I was feeling filtering through.

"It gives her someone to chase when she gets old enough. We don't need another teenage going head-to-head with Jackson before she's trained enough to be successful."

"I escaped," I mumbled. It felt like her teenager comment was just a little pointed at me.

Ally nodded. "And that is why I think Jackson won't hesitate to come for you after I die. You humiliated him and the Circle of Fifths. If word gets out that you survived an attack from them, *and* escaped their custody, it ruins their credibility just as much as what Alyx has done."

I thought about what Ally had said for a moment. Having Vee identify them and do the damage she'd done at only five-years old was embarrassing, but could be written off as a fluke.

What I'd done…not so much.

I knew I was well trained, and had been training for twelve years—that I could remember. But the Circle of Fifths didn't see me as an almost-adult with more experience than the majority of their agents. They saw me as an unimportant minor who had bested several of their top agents.

Not even any of the New Generation agents had been able to come close.

That made me a threat.

"I won't just give up a future in espionage, especially when I've already come so close to defeating them," I told Ally.

"I don't think mom will be able to handle it—"

"Let me finish, please," I interrupted. "I agree with you. If I join the agency as soon as I turn eighteen in five months, I won't last a week, and that won't help me take them down.

"What are you thinking?" Ally asked me.

I loved that she knew me so well. It wasn't a question about whether or not I had a solution. She knew I had one, and she was asking I share my idea with her.

Man, I was going to miss her.

Before I got lost in my grief for my not-yet-dead sister, I decided to tell her my idea.

"I already have one asset inside the Circle of Fifths with Elisabeth. I'm guessing based on what you've told me, you and I are the only ones who will still know Rafael is on our side. If he is ok with it, I can take over running him as an asset."

"That doesn't help you stay hidden from the Circle of Fifths," Ally stated.

I shook my head. "I don't have to be CIA to run them as assets. In fact, it would probably be better if I wasn't. I have already been applying to schools in California. I was thinking I wanted to study Criminal Justice at UC Irvine, but have been looking at Computer Science programs as well. Either way, I can do that while I run the Promising Generation. Their servers are completely separate from the agency's, which means I would have a secure division to run my assets, store intelligence, and hunt the Circle of Fifths."

Ally nodded. "You have a solid plan. What about Carlyle?"

I sighed. William and I were already planning on transferring George to make sure the Promising Generation was Circle of Fifths-free. But Carlyle's current entrenchment in the Promising Generation meant any current plans for the Generation needed to be changed *after* he was transferred.

"We can't used the school," I said when I realized it. "Carlyle is going to be transferred, but he knows too much about current operations."

I started pacing at the foot of Ally's hospital bed, letting my mind work through the various possibilities.

"It would probably be best to move them, after Carlyle's transfer. If I can have him sign Peter's custody over to the Generation, that would mean I wouldn't have to notify him of the change, but I'd like to stay in California, since I've already applied to schools there. The problem is UC Irvine is the only school with a Criminal Justice degree. I could choose one of my back-ups I applied to in Northern California…" I rambled.

"Applications are open until the end of the month, correct?" Ally asked me.

"Yeah, November 30th. Why?" I replied.

"Do more research on Computer Science programs. You are fascinated by computers, and you're more than proficient using them. Plus it will help you set up the Generation servers so that they're more secure than the CIA's."

Ally laid her head back on the pillows and closed her eyes.

"What are you doing?" I asked concerned. "Are you ok? Do I need to call a nurse."

"I'm fine," Ally complained, her eyes still closed. "I'm just tired, and it seems I was concerned about your future for no reason. The Circle of Fifths should be terrified, but you're not going to warn them."

"I learned from the best," I told her as I sat back down next to her bed, taking her hand in mine.

Ally gave me a small smile as she squeezed my hand, while her eyes remained closed.

"I don't know how I'm going to handle this without you being there to give me advice," I admitted. The tears I'd been holding back for days finally falling.

Ally's eyes shot open. "Look at me," she demanded.

So I did.

"You are more than capable of everything you laid out, and you have a solid plan. Listen to your instincts, and don't let anyone else tell you you're not capable. Not me, not Sarah, not Dylan, not Michael, not William, and not even mom."

"Ok," I replied.

"Promise me," Ally said.

"I promise." And I meant it.

"Good," Ally said, reclosing her eyes.

So I just sat there in silence, holding my sister's hand, appreciating the time I had to spend with her.

"Oh, after my funeral, find Thomas," Ally said, her voice slurred, probably because she was on the verge of sleep.

"Why?" I asked quietly.

"Tell him you know about Rafael and Cole. He will know you're the one who is inheriting those secrets," Ally told me.

"I will," I promised softly, returning us to silence.

As Ally's breathing deepened, and formed a rhythmic pattern, I knew she'd fallen asleep.

I let silent tears fall as I mourned my sister, and the legacy of secrets she left behind.

TOP SECRET PROMISING GENERATION EYES ONLY

Operation Subversion
Objective: Systematically dismantle the Circle of Fifths

FIELD REPORT:23 November 2000

CLASSIFIED TOP SECRET

13:07 GMT Feilds Cemetery; Twickenham, London
20:53 GMT Lincoln Avenue; Twickenham, London

Thursday

13:07 GMT
Twickenham, London
Fields Cemetery

AS CLICHE AS IT IS, it rained on the day of the funeral. Then again, it was Fall in England. There hadn't been many days in the almost three weeks I'd been here it *hadn't* been raining. If I hadn't known better, I might have been tempted to believe the weather was being controlled by my mood.

It was most definitely a reflection of it.

Aside from the rain, the funeral last Saturday had been the loving tribute Ally deserved, and seeing our family gathered around the graveside was a testament to how much she was loved and would be missed. It was clear some of the kids didn't understand, like Kate, who I'd heard ask for her mom more than once during the service.

But Alyx? My sweet little niece Vee understood *perfectly* what the service meant, because she had already attended too many funerals in her short life.

It was clear Vee was sad, but she could tell others were even more sad than she was, so she'd provided comfort to others. She had stood right next to her three-year-old cousin, holding Kate's hand, and distracting her if she ever got too sad. I'd even seen Vee wipe the tears from Sarah's face, and tell her Ally was watching over them with Cole and Annie.

As I walked to the pile of fresh dirt that marked Ally's grave, I wished I could borrow some of Vee's strength. I hadn't been back to Ally's grave since the service. My brother and sister had. My mom had come here everyday since the funeral. But I hadn't been able to bring myself here yet. It just felt so final, and I wasn't ready for that. The only reason I was here now was because we were flying home tomorrow, and I knew I wouldn't be coming back to London anytime soon.

This was my last chance I'd have for a while to visit Ally's grave.

I laid the bouquet of white flowers I'd found on top of the dirt—just more flowers on a pile of others in various stages of wilting.

When I was little, and Michael was courting Ally long distance, she'd once commented to me that her biggest complaint about the distance was the fact that she would never get flowers *just because*. She had never really cared what kind, as long as they were white. She *loved* white flowers. If I remembered right, she loved the fact that nature was able to make something so pure.

Now she had all the white flowers she wanted.

"This sucks," I commented out loud. "It's not fair you had to die for us to buy you flowers."

I sighed. Talking to a grave is weird. Did I just say things I wished I could say to her? Or would it be better to make up a conversation between the two of us?

For the first time in my life, I could actually win an argument with Ally if I did that.

I thought back to the conversation I'd had with her in the hospital. We hadn't been arguing, but we definitely hadn't seen eye-to-eye about my future. Yet, by the end of our conversation, I'd convinced Ally that my idea would work. If she had lived, how many more arguments could I have won?

"We're doing Thanksgiving with Michael, Thomas, and Kate this year," I told her. "Mom, Sarah, and Addi are showing Michael how to prepare your favorite: Cranberry Fluff. That man is in way over his head, but is dedicated to giving Kate a way to remember you."

After Ally died, and we scheduled her funeral for last Saturday, we decided to stay through Thanksgiving. For those of us still in school, we weren't missing any more school, and it gave us time to spend as a family not at a hospital or funeral. Truthfully, I couldn't remember the last time my family was together for Thanksgiving…

Mom was an immigrant, so she hadn't had any family Thanksgiving traditions when she married dad as it was an American holiday. It had been dad's favorite holiday though, so he'd always made a big deal of it for us kids growing up. Since mom hadn't grown up with the holiday, dad decided to get the entire family involved in preparing Thanksgiving dinner. He'd never particularly cared for the idea of the women cooking all day while the men watched football, and mom gave him the opportunity to redefine the holiday for our family.

Once we were old enough, each of us chose our favorite dish, and learned how to cook it. Dad always cooked the Turkey, which he insisted was a must, no matter what the rest of us decided to make. I'd heard stories about some truly weird Thanksgiving meals before I was born, but as long as I could remember, everyone made the same things: Ally made Cranberry Fluff, Sarah made Crêpes (and despite sounding weird, they were surprisingly good filled with Turkey and gravy), Dylan made Green Bean Casserole, and I helped mom make Tarte Tatin.

Our Thanksgiving dinners definitely weren't like any of our classmates, but it was our tradition—a combination of our parents' cultures.

Thanksgiving was harder to do after Sarah, then Dylan, and eventually Ally got married. Dad still dragged mom to California, and tried to guilt all of my siblings into coming home. Ally rarely made it. Then dad died. Mom withdrew. The family tradition didn't exactly die with dad, but it wasn't the same.

Today we were teaching Michael about our family tradition, so he could keep it alive for Kate, including Ally's favorite dish.

Michael was a good father. It was clear he loved Ally with his entire heart, and when Kate had been born, that love somehow grew to include Kate. He would do just about anything for his little girl. That meant he wasn't going to let his devastation from losing the love of his life prevent his daughter from knowing her mother. In fact, it had been his idea to do a traditional Hall Thanksgiving. Apparently he'd read about it in Ally's journal.

When she first moved to London, she'd been terribly homesick, but hadn't wanted to tell Michael about it. She didn't want him to think she resented him for taking her away from her family, because she didn't. She also didn't want him to feel guilty. So she used a journal to process her feelings of home sickness and hid it away.

The journal had been the secret Michael inherited from Ally. She'd told him about it in the hospital so he would have something he could give to Kate when she got older to remember her mom by.

I sighed, thinking again about my conversation with Ally at the hospital. "I applied to UC Davis," I told Ally. "They have a really good Computer Science program, and it will take me about seven hours away from where the Circle of Fifths would think to look for me."

I was honestly pretty excited to attend UC Davis. It might not have been anywhere near where I grew up, but that just meant it was an opportunity for a fresh start, and after the last couple of weeks, I needed one of those. No one would know me or my family, and I could create a whole new persona for myself.

All I could hope was that I figured out my new persona soon, and it included a good cover career to hide my espionage activities.

"You look like she did," a male voice with a British accent said from behind me. "You are too young to have the weight of your family secrets on your shoulders."

"Someone had to inherit her burdens," I replied. I turned away from Ally's grave to face Michael's father, Lord Thomas Fields. William stood next to him, and if I hadn't known both of them, I'm not sure I would have noticed the subtle differences in their dress that differentiated which one was the American, and which one was the Englishman.

"That doesn't mean I agree it should have been you," Thomas complained.

"I'm perfectly capable—" I started to argue.

"I never meant to suggest otherwise," Thomas interrupted. "I simply believe you should have been allowed more time to enjoy the exploits of childhood before being weighed down by the worries of adulthood."

I shrugged. "We don't get to decide when the call will come, only whether or not to answer it."

"Emily and I have already had a version of this conversation," William told Thomas. "You won't convince her to wait. She thinks even the few months before she turns eighteen is too long to wait."

"Stubborn, is she?" Thomas said.

"Just like her father," William confirmed.

I didn't know Thomas knew my dad too. Made sense, I guess.

"And based on the report she wrote about the mission she and Ally embarked on, I would say she is even more stubborn than Ally."

Thomas muttered something I didn't quite catch under his breath, before sighing, "Very well. I gather, based on your comments,

Ally passed on some of her secrets to you."

I nodded. "Two of them. And because William debriefed me after California, he knows them as well."

"I don't care who you share Ally's secrets with, as long as you remember—"

"I know. I might not agree with all of them, but I will not share them further than this group," I promised.

Thomas nodded. "Which secrets did she leave you?"

"Rafael and Cole," I told him.

Thomas glanced between William and I. "Rafael's loyalties are not what they once were."

"You might be surprised," I said. "I know more than you might think. Like the fact that you had Rafael under surveillance here in London when Ally was supposed to meet with him in Moscow."

Thomas raised an eyebrow.

"Rafael's trip to LA was to help Ally rescue me. Doing so jeopardized his cover, so Ally took a risk to help him secure it." I explained. "It worked, but he is unhappy with the cost."

"You are in contact with my son," Thomas said.

"I am," I replied, even though it hadn't really been a question.

Thomas looked at William, who just shrugged. "Don't ask me. I let Ally take her to California, and she turned two assets, convinced Ally to go home, went head-to-head with the assassin that killed one of her assets, escaped, identified Ally's compromised phone line, made it across the US by herself, then correctly identified Ally's kidnappers. If I would have let her, she would have flown to Russia to rescue Ally herself."

"When you put it like that, you make it sound more impressive than it was," I mumbled.

"I'm still struggling to believe Ally told her about Rafael," Thomas admitted.

"She didn't. Rafael told me as we drove into New Mexico," I corrected.

"Then how do you know you can trust him, and he wasn't lying to you?" Thomas asked.

"I was with them at the safehouse when he supposedly turned," I reminded them. "And he called me when Ally missed her check in. I don't care how good of an actor he is; the pure panic in his voice isn't something that can be faked. The timing of his call, and how many times he tried to reach me speaks volumes as well."

"So your sister was lying when she said Rafael was the one responsible?" Thomas asked.

"Eh," I said, trying to give myself time to think about how to answer. "Ally knew she was walking into a trap. Rafael didn't betray her. He also wasn't the one who kidnapped or poisoned her. Ally talked to Rafael after Nika rescued her, and he agreed—"

"Nika didn't rescue Ally," Thomas interrupted. "She showed up, by herself, at our embassy in Moscow."

"One can be true without disproving the other," William commented. "After I verified that there was unauthorized use of a CIA safehouse, I needed someone in the country to alert the authorities, and Nika seemed like someone they would trust. I'm sure you can see, however, why Ally would need to show up at the embassy alone."

Thomas sighed. "The doctors said it was a miracle that she escaped in her condition. I suppose it makes sense she was rescued…"

If I wasn't mistaken, Thomas appeared to finally be letting himself have the tiniest bit of hope for Rafael.

"Why did she and Rafael agree he should take credit for her death?" Thomas asked.

"That's what they need the official reports to say for two reasons. First, it solidifies his cover with the Circle of Fifths. Second, when Alyx and the others are old enough to chase Ally's killer, it gives them someone safe to chase, so they don't end up face-to-face with Jackson like I did," I explained.

"Her plan sounds doomed to fail," Thomas complained. "I can already see one main flaw."

"Which is?" William asked.

"Keeping Rafael's help in Ally's case out of the official report means he will become an off-the-books operative. MI-6 will have no choice but to label him a terrorist, which means he will lose our resources and support."

"Maybe from MI-6, or even the CIA. But he has plenty of resources on his own. We just need to change who he reports to," I reasoned.

"You wouldn't be suggesting he reports to his wife, would you? Nika might help us on occasion, and things with the Russians are better than they were ten years ago, but they're in no way friendly," Thomas said.

"Not Nika. Me," I said. "Rafael has already agreed with the change."

"Running him as an asset through the CIA is even more dangerous than MI-6," Thomas exclaimed.

I shook my head. "I'm not joining the CIA when I turn 18."

"Then how do you plan on running an asset?" Thomas asked.

"The Promising Generation," I replied.

Thomas looked at William for an explanation. Clearly he didn't understand what I'd said, which was fair. Why would he have heard of our training experiment in California?

"It's a privately-owned training program. Sarah recruited agents with children to join her task-force hunting the Circle of Fifths in LA. Those kids, including me, were then given the option to join the Promising Generation. We have private servers to maintain the children's privacy."

"Sarah signed control over to me, and I will sign control over to Emily when she turns eighteen. She has already negotiated for a government contract to supplement funding, and give the organization legitimacy while maintaining autonomy," William told Thomas.

"How can you be sure it won't be infiltrated by the Circle of Fifths?" Thomas asked.

"We can't, just like we can't be sure they won't infiltrate MI-6, or any task force we put together to go after them," I admitted. "What I can tell you is I have an asset who has made sure I found and extricated the moles currently in the program."

Thomas didn't look too assured of our security, which was to be expected.

I shrugged. "I *am* the only one with access to the files at the moment, and I don't foresee giving one of the members access without a thorough background check."

That was more true than my casual demeanor about it might suggest. I had already negotiated with William to have a certified psychologist from the training division assigned as the liaison between the CIA and the Promising Generation. Despite his assignment and the extensive checks we'd done (including a rather uncomfortable conversation between him and Elisabeth Stevens), he had clearance to offer the members of the Promising Generation counseling, but he could not read their files himself. He'd agreed to our conditions, and whether that was because he didn't care to know, or because I offered him the same courtesy as it pertained to his psychological evaluations, I didn't know.

Thomas nodded, "Ok. You better keep my son safe."

"I will," I promised.

What was another promise on an ever climbing mountain of promises and secrets I was responsible for.

Now for the second secret I inherited. "I know Cole likely

would like to stay here, but can I see him before I leave? I would like him to know he's not alone."

"I will arrange that for you. We can go after this dinner," Thomas replied.

"Speaking of which," William said, "Sarah sent us to come get you. We should get back before she sends the search parties."

Thomas offered his arm, which I took, and we started walking back to Fields Palace.

William squoze my shoulder as Thomas walked us into the large kitchen which was usually reserved for the chefs the Fields family employed. Their head chef hadn't been particularly thrilled when Michael told him we were taking over this kitchen. Usually, when the family gave their staff the day off, they used the smaller family kitchen, and while our Hall family tradition always made-do with a kitchen smaller than the Fields family kitchen, it was *really* nice not trying to fight over one oven to cook our dishes.

"Look who we found," William announced.

I rolled my eyes, rejoining my mom as she checked the Tarte Tatin in the oven.

20:53 GMT
Twickenham, London
Lincoln Avenue

THE TOWN CAR CAME TO a stop in front of a quaint family home. It hadn't taken too long for us to get here from Fields Palace, which told me Ally had chosen this house for a reason. It was far enough away that the chances were slim someone who would recognize Cole saw him, but still close enough that help wasn't too far away.

"We'll be done at 9:30," Thomas told his driver.

"Understood," the driver replied.

Thomas opened his door and climbed out, so I did the same. As we walked up to the house, I couldn't help but notice the fact that the garden looked like children played in it often, unlike the well tended-to gardens of Fields Palace.

"Hannah and Oliver are expecting us," Thomas told me as we reached the door. "They don't know him as Cole, nor that he is related to Ally."

"Ally arranged a new identity for him?" I asked.

"Yes," Thomas replied. "Cole McLean died, so he is now Stephan Cross, an orphan who just lost his parents and sisters."

Stephan Cross. It was a decent name. Hopefully it wasn't too hard for me to remember, so I could keep an eye on him from the states.

We reached the door, and Thomas knocked softly.

"Oh, and Emily, one last thing…"

"Yes?" I asked.

"Michael doesn't know about any of the secrets you're about to see. Ally and I were the only two who knew *all* of the secrets in this house. Now, so will you."

"I understand," I replied, the implication clear.

This house didn't contain state secrets, but if it did, they would be Classified Top Secret, and Thomas had the sole discretion who got access.

It made me a little nervous for what I was about to see.

A woman around Sarah and Ally's age opened the door, her red hair pulled back into a bun. She bowed her head Thomas. "Lord Fields," she greeted.

"Operative Cross," Thomas said in return. "This is Stephan's cousin, Emily. Is he still awake?"

The woman nodded. "He is. I'll let him know you are here."

She opened the door wider and stepped to the side. "Would you like to come in?"

"Thank you," Thomas replied, stepping through the door.

I took a deep breath then followed him into the world of Ally's secrets.

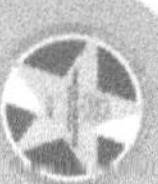

TOP SECRET PROMISING GENERATION EYES ONLY

Operation Subversion
Objective: Systematically dismantle the Circle of Fifths

FIELD REPORT: 20 August 2001

CLASSIFIED TOP SECRET

14:32 PDT UC Davis Main Campus; Sacramento, CA

14:32 PDT
Sacramento, CA
UC Davis Main Campus

I GLANCED AWAY FROM THE screen of my iBook to grab my water bottle and take a drink of the ice water it contained. I had a break between classes, and had already eaten, so I'd decided to finish up my report of the conversation I'd had with Elisabeth this morning. I had done a pretty good job of writing reports as things happened even though I hadn't been able to access the Promising Generation servers from Virginia, and I was glad I had. After I graduated, I took a trip back to LA to link my laptop to the server, and uploaded the reports I'd been writing. It took me maybe a couple of days to upload Cole's report, the report about what happened in California and Vegas last Fall, and the weekly reports I wrote when Elisabeth checked-in. I had also updated Cole's codename file to show his new name. If someone looked close enough, they might figure out Stephan Cross was Cole McLean, but by the time I gave a member of the Generation access, I doubted they'd remember Cole, never mind care enough to check.

If I hadn't kept up on the reports, it would have taken me all summer to update the Operation Subversion file.

Instead, William was able to help me find a house close enough to UC Davis I could live there if I wanted to, but not too close it was easy to follow me. We'd found a nice new development in a city called Tracy about an hour south of where I was attending school, I'd chosen a lot and a floor plan, and put a deposit down on the house. William had arranged for the builders to add a hidden basement for the Promising Generation Servers, which would be moved with the kids once the house was finished.

Now, I could start school without any overwhelming administrative tasks for the Promising Generation looming over me.

"Care if we join you?" someone asked.

I looked up at the young men who were standing next to me, their arms carefully balancing Forensic Science text books and a plate with a slice of pizza.

"Sorry to disturb you, it's just, this is the only open seat, and we really need to eat before our next lab," the young man added.

I nodded, condensing my own textbook pile to give them space. Honestly, I would have preferred they didn't join me. I had quite a bit to add from Elisabeth's check-in, and didn't really need the distraction if I wanted to get it done before my next class, but he was right. There wasn't anywhere else to go, and I wasn't going to be rude and insist they find another seat with how full their arms were.

The young men sat down. The quieter one gave me a smile of gratitude, then true to their word, they began eating quietly, trying not to distract me.

Too bad their mere presence was more than distracting enough.

Despite taking detailed notes this morning, I was distracted enough I couldn't remember any of my conversation with Elisabeth, and I knew there were some important things I needed to do this week to convince George Carlyle to transfer and leave Peter in the care of the Promising Generation. Yet, for whatever reason, I couldn't concentrate for more than a couple of seconds before I found my eyes glancing over the top of my laptop to watch the quiet stranger eat.

Man, that sounded so creepy.

"Is there something on my face, computer science?"

"Computer Science?" I asked.

He nodded, pointing to my books. "I'm assuming that's your major based on the textbooks."

"So, what? You're just going to dehumanize me and call me by my major? I have a name, forensic science." I retorted, any attraction I may have felt was fading as my anger grew. *Let's see how he feels about being broken down to nothing but his area of study.*

Forensic Science smirked—*actually smirked*—at me, like it didn't bother him in the slightest.

What a self-centered—

"You're deflecting," his friend commented.

"*What?*"

His irritating smirk stayed glued on his annoyingly perfect lips. "I caught you staring, and instead of admitting it so I could ask for your gorgeous name, since I'm sure it matches you, you found something to be outraged over," Forensic Science explained.

Was this guy *flirting?* With *me?*

I knew I'd been ostracized by my classmates in Virginia, but I didn't think it had been so long since I'd had normal conversations with people my age that I'd forgotten what flirting looked like.

It didn't matter now. I was too embarrassed. Even if he was flirting, I'd never be able to face him again.

I shut my laptop, the clamshell clicking shut before I placed it in my laptop bag that I'd retrieved from by my feet.

Time to admit defeat and leave.

"Hey, wait up," the friend called, running after me. "I'm sorry about Jack. He's… an acquired taste. And I didn't mean to call you out for not answering his question. It's just that I got my undergraduate degree in psychology… and I'm rambling. Let's start over."

I turned to look at him as he extended his hand in the ultimate gesture of wishing to introduce himself.

"I'm Bryan Ryneholt. Like Jack, I'm getting my Masters in Forensic Science," he told me. "Unlike Jack, I know better than to give strangers nicknames, so what's your name?"

I took his hand, giving him the quick, firm handshake I'd practiced over the years. "Emily Hall."

As I gave him my name, it felt impactful and important. For what ever reason, I felt like I was starting the rest of my life.

Acknowledgements

THIS BOOK HAS BEEN A labor of love that would not exist without the support of several people over the last ten years.

First, I'd like to thank my sister Mikayli, who has played the role of, and in many ways inspired, the sassy queen that is Emily Hall. We may make fun of our youngest sister for being the stereotypical spoiled youngest child, but you have truly been the unsung hero of our family, quietly pulling us all together in a way only you could. You are the best confidant any sibling could ask for; I couldn't have done this without you as my real-life underestimated baby sister.

Thank you Patrice for encouraging you kids to read, and letting me give my books and their drafts to your daughter…even if the cliffhangers and my slow writing process dictate her mood for weeks. And to your daughter, the best beta reader in the world—Thank you for sharing all of your excitement, feedback, and theories with me. You remind me constantly why I do this, and show me what it's like to figure out and discover the secrets of this world for the first time, since I've lost that excitement after hundreds of drafts.

I would be remiss if I didn't acknowledge Professor Lepa Marinkovski (one of my college professors), who encouraged me to look at the Prom Gen Files from a new POV, and let me tell teenaged Emily's story for the final assignment in Adolescent Lit. That short story became the outline for this book, and gave me the courage to tell Emily's story in first person.

Thank you to my coworkers, who let me talk their ears off about this book so I could figure out how to move past the writer's block. To my mangers, thank you for being flexible with my schedule so I could find time to finish this book.

To Ambri and Lauryn, thank you for helping me figure out how to start this book. Getting this prequel just right was stressful, and you helped me get out of my head to FINALLY start writing it.

Last but not least, Thank you for reading this book. Your support of me as an author and story teller means the world. I hope you enjoy the twists and turns of Emily Hall's story as much as I do.

www.ingramcontent.com/pod-product-compliance
Lightning Source LLC
Chambersburg PA
CBHW010447310726
48979CB00018B/2841/J

* 9 7 8 1 9 5 5 1 9 2 0 8 8 *